AMANDA

illustrated by Sheila Greenwald

AMANDA

by Ruth Loomis

New York   THE MACMILLAN COMPANY   1962

A Division of the Crowell-Collier Publishing Company

Library of Congress catalog card number: 62-8157

First Printing

The Macmillan Company, New York
Brett-Macmillan Ltd., Galt, Ontario
Printed in the United States of America

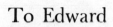
To Edward

Contents

1　Amanda Arrives

"Get down from that wall!"

Liz looked up and down the wall, which was unoccupied except for herself and her sister. The voice from the window could only have been directed at them, but it was not the voice her mother used for serious occasions, and so Liz decided to pretend she hadn't heard it. She glanced at Keechie, but Keechie had heard nothing.

The two girls sat on the highest section of the brick wall that enclosed their back yard. From it, they commanded a splendid view. They could see not only the front and back yards of the house next door but all the way down West Jefferson to the corner of their block. They could be found on the wall at some time on almost every day. They watched the milkman making his rounds and the postman bicycling on his way, and their knowledge of the comings and goings of their neighbors was precise and detailed.

At the moment the scene was particularly interesting. The house next door was being occupied by a new tenant, and Liz and Keechie were watching the movers unload the huge moving van parked in the driveway. They already knew a great deal about the new people. There was a father who had a beard and gave loud directions; there was a small boy who kept getting in the way; and there was a mother who couldn't seem to remember where she was. She would come running out of the house to snatch the boy up from under someone's feet; then she would stop with her chin in her hand, and Liz could hear her say, "Now, where was I?" There was also a big girl who appeared once in the doorway to exchange an indifferent stare with Liz and Keechie. There was a pink-striped rocking chair and a sofa that came apart in the middle and a dressing table with a mirror that was bigger than Keechie.

"Lookie," Keechie said. "What's that?" The movers had just brought a large piano out of the van and were maneuvering to get it in the door.

"It's a piano, Keechie." Liz turned to her brother who was at work in their back yard. "Tom," she called, "they have a piano."

Tom didn't look up from the orange crate he was

systematically breaking up into its original pieces. "So what," he said. "Lots of people have a piano."

"Well, we don't," Liz said defensively. Behind her, Liz heard the door open and her mother come out into the yard.

"Liz and Keechie, did you hear me?" This time Liz knew her mother was in earnest. "Get down from that wall!"

"But, Mama, then we won't be able to see," Liz said.

"It's most impolite to stare that way." Liz's mother was holding a baby bottle in her hand and impatiently shaking drops against her wrist to test the temperature of the milk while she waited for Liz and Keechie to obey her.

"They have a pilano, Mommy," Keechie said.

"A what?"

"A piano," Liz said. "But they don't have any TV."

"It's none of our business what they have. Now get down, Keechie, before you break your neck."

With Liz behind her, Keechie began to crawl slowly along the wall toward the pepper tree that branched out over the wall. She had not gone four feet before she froze.

"I can't," Keechie wailed. Inside the house, Liz heard her baby brother, Mike, begin to cry.

"Then how in the world did you get up there?" Liz watched her mother hesitate between her crying baby and her stranded daughter, and saw the baby win.

"Tom, will you help Keechie down? I have to feed Mike."

"Okay, Mom." Tom continued to collect the nails he had salvaged from the orange crate.

"*Now*," Liz's mother said, and turned and went back into the house. Tom did not move from his work.

"Come on, Keechie." Liz crawled backward to the stretch of wall that she knew could not be seen from any of the windows in their house. Keechie, suddenly overcoming her fear, crawled after her and sat close beside her sister. The two girls happily kicked their heels against the wall.

"You better get down or I'll tell Mom," Tom said. Liz knew that Tom was too busy to bother about them, and ignored the threat.

The job next door seemed to be finished. There was no more activity outside. The girls waited patiently, but when the movers finally reappeared they closed up their van, and drove off. Saddened, Liz and Keechie watched the van disappear around the corner.

"Where's the TV, Lizzie?" Keechie said finally. "I wonder."

"We haven't one." The strange voice spoke from close beside them. Liz turned in surprise, and saw that they were no longer alone on the wall. They had been joined by the new girl from next door. She sat with her legs dangling easily on their side of the wall as if she had been watching Tom for a long time. Liz looked at her enviously. Her hair was cut short and it curled in soft rings all over her head. Liz desperately wanted curls, but her mother refused to cut off her pony tail.

"Why is your ear so green?" Keechie stared at the girl, and Liz stared too. Peeping out from under her hair was a bright green tip of ear. Liz poked Keechie, and said, "Ss-hh," but the girl didn't seem to be offended. She didn't even look at them.

"Oh, it always does that when we move on Wednesday," she said indifferently.

"Doesn't your mother put cold cream on it?" Liz looked concerned.

"Mostly she doesn't notice."

Liz could think of nothing more to say, and the girls sat in silence until Keechie reopened the conversation.

"I'm going to have my happy birthday pretty soon," she said. "You can come." Liz was embarrassed by Keechie's boldness, but the girl turned and stared at Keechie solemnly.

"Thank you," she said. "I will."

"I'm going to be . . ." Keechie stopped, and began a series of complicated manipulations with her fingers. She held up three fingers and looked at them closely. "Six," she announced.

"No," Liz said. "I'm six. You're going to be three."

"Three," Keechie said. "Are you six . . . or three?"

"Neither," the girl scoffed, and lost interest in them. She turned her attention back to Tom, who was now hammering the slats from the orange crate onto the end of a wooden barrel. Liz looked too and thought it was really one of the nicest of Tom's constructions, better even than the Ferris wheel he had made with his Tinker Toys. There were two wooden barrels attached together with old boards, as well as a great deal of wire and assorted tin cans. With some indignation, Liz recognized the wheels from her broken doll buggy, and on the front she saw the straw hat that her mother had given her for playing dress-up. The construction was mounted on two sawhorses. The new girl watched Tom a long time before she spoke again.

"What's he doing?"

"Building," Liz said eagerly. "He's always building something. Mama says we might as well live behind the dump."

The girl didn't answer. She got up and walked along the wall until she came to the pepper tree. She swung down to the branch that extended above the wall, and dropped into their yard. Keechie and Liz crawled along the wall behind her. When Keechie reached the tree, she stood on one branch, holding onto the one above, and inched her way along to the trunk. From there the branches made an easy ladder to the ground. Liz considered swinging down but decided against it and followed Keechie. They went with the new girl over to stand near Tom. He took no notice of them.

"What's that?" the girl asked.

6

"A rocket," Tom said. "I'm going to shoot it to the moon."

"It'll never make it."

"What do you know about it?" Tom asked angrily.

The girl shrugged and went over to sit on the swing that hung from the pepper tree. Tom went into the house and came back with a can opener. He began to take the tops and bottoms off the empty tin cans he had lined up beside one of the sawhorses. He had opened six cans before he spoke.

"What's wrong with it?"

"In the first place the wetzel's all wrong," the girl said.

"It is not!" Tom was indignant.

"Then," the girl said, "if you don't balance the borsnerd with the belsnord, you'll never manage the ganinuclear pull."

"There's nothing wrong with the wetzel," Tom maintained.

The girl shrugged again and turned around on the swing to sit with her back to Tom. She looked at Keechie, who was whimpering.

"What's wrong with her?"

"She wants a pretzel," Liz said.

"Oh." The girl reached down into the pocket of her skirt and brought out a pretzel and handed it to Keechie.

"Well, say," Tom began, "how would you go about

balancing the bolsnord with the — ah — the belsnerd?"

Very slowly, the girl got up and walked over to the rocket. She circled it twice; she tapped it several times; she peered inside; she knelt down and looked at the bottom. Then she nodded slowly.

"I think it could be done, all right," she said. "Actually it's not a bad idea. It would never work this way, but I think you could fix it up."

"Ah, nuts," Tom said. "What do you know about rockets?"

Liz winced. She was sure that the girl would be offended and go away. But the girl ignored Tom; she merely walked around the rocket again, and nodded.

"Let's see," she said. "We'll need hairpins and a tube of toothpaste, a box of baking soda, a ruler, and a pair of silk stockings. You," she pointed to Tom, "go get those." Tom looked at her in disgust. "Or can't you remember that much?"

"Of course I can remember," Tom said, and went off into the house.

"You, Liz," the girl said, "go fill those buckets in the sandbox up with sand and bring them over here. And Keechie, you go get a cammaguppy."

Watching Keechie doubtfully, Liz backed toward the sandbox. Keechie got the wagon and disappeared around the front of the house, pulling the wagon behind her. While Liz filled the buckets, she watched the new girl inspecting Tom's work. She tapped at it and smelled it and even put her ear against it to listen. Often she shook her head disapprovingly; once or twice she nodded wisely. Liz was back first. When Keechie and Tom returned, the girl put them all to work. She set out a row of cans for Liz and told her to fill them all with sand. She gave the tube of toothpaste to Keechie and told her to stand on the wagon so that she could reach inside the last barrel. Balanced on tiptoe, Keechie got her head and arms and shoulders inside the barrel.

"It's dark in here."

"That's all right," the girl said. "Just smear the toothpaste on and smooth it over."

The girl took the ruler from Tom and made a series of careful measurements. Then she pointed out to Tom which boards he was to remove.

"I don't know what you think you're doing," Tom said.

"First," the girl explained, "we're going to fix the forward list and equalize the thermofund."

Liz spooned out her sand slowly. She was just finishing when Keechie came out of the barrel, proudly holding an empty tube of toothpaste. She sat down beside Liz and sucked on the empty tube. They watched Tom and the new girl work and listened to them argue. Liz worried because the new girl's mouth was full of hairpins and Tom's mouth was full of nails, and Liz was sure that one of them was going

to swallow something. The mumbled argument finally reached a climax, and Tom threw down his hammer, spat out his mouthful of nails, and walked off contemptuously.

"Good," the girl said. "That about does it. You," she called to Tom, "stay back there at a safe distance, and I'll close it up." Tom turned indignantly, but she waved him back and pushed Liz and Keechie over beside him. Then, very carefully, the girl closed up the end of the rocket. When she had finished, she came over and stood with them.

"There," she said. "Now, don't any of you touch it. And if I were you"—she looked at Tom—"I'd fire it off pretty soon before anyone gets hurt."

"Is it dangerous?" Liz asked.

"Naw," Tom said. "It's just old boards and tin cans."

"There'll be a full moon tonight," the girl said. "If you fire now, you'll hit it about nine o'clock. When the moon's just over the pepper tree."

Tom looked at her disgustedly. "You really think you're going to hit the moon with that?"

The girl didn't bother to answer. She licked her finger and held it up to test the wind. "All right," she said. "I'll do it." She reached into her pocket and took out a pack of matches. She warned them all back another two feet, struck a match, and delicately touched it to the end of the rocket.

There was a tremendous explosion. A great cloud of white smoke billowed up around the girl. When the

smoke cleared, Liz saw her standing with her hand still upraised, gazing at the sky beyond the empty sawhorses. Liz didn't have time to follow her look. The back door banged, and their mother rushed into the yard.

"What was that?" she cried. "What happened?"

The new girl turned and looked at her calmly. "Oh, those movers," she said. "I told them to be careful with my chemistry set."

Liz's mother gaped at the new girl. Then she looked toward the house next door, but all was quiet there.

"I'm Amanda Cook," the girl said. "I'm going to live next door. I'm very pleased to meet you." She approached Liz's mother and held out her hand.

Liz's mother fumbled for a moment, then took Amanda's hand.

"Well," she said. "I'm very pleased to meet you, Amanda. I'm Mrs. Dunn." She looked past Amanda at her children, who turned their blank faces toward her. "I guess you know the children already." She looked nervously from one to another, and Liz wondered what was wrong with her mother. "Well," Mrs. Dunn said, "as long as nobody's hurt . . ." and hurried back into the house.

Without looking at any of them, Amanda walked toward the pepper tree. "Nine o'clock," she said. "Give or take about five minutes." She swung up to the wall and dropped down on her own side.

Liz hurried Keechie through their bath that night. She allowed her to have the largest bar of soap and even washed the bottoms of Keechie's feet where her mother always checked. They were already out of the tub when Mrs. Dunn came in to hurry them. Without prompting, they brushed their teeth, got into their pajamas, and were in bed when their mother came back.

"What book do you want tonight, dears?"

"We don't want a book, Mama," Liz said.

"Why, what's the matter?"

"Nothing. We're just sleepy."

"Do you feel all right?"

"Yes, Mama." Liz yawned.

Mrs. Dunn put her hand on Liz's forehead and then on Keechie's. "You're quite sure?" she asked. "You don't seem to have any fever."

"We're just sleepy, Mama," Liz said.

"All right." Mrs. Dunn kissed them and left the room shaking her head.

Liz listened to her mother go into Tom's room, then to Mike's room, and finally downstairs. Even after all was quiet on the second floor, she waited a long time. Then she climbed down from her bed and shook Keechie gently.

"Come on," she whispered.

Still half asleep, Keechie got up and took her hand. They crept down the hall to their brother's room. The

13

door was open, and Liz saw Tom standing by the window.

"Tom," Liz said. Tom jumped guiltily and hurried to his desk. "Tom, what time is it?"

"How should I know?"

"Is it nine o'clock?"

"That's all nonsense," Tom said. "Don't bother me about it."

Liz led Keechie back to their room and pulled the chair up in front of the window. The two girls sat on the arm, and waited. They watched the moon slowly climbing until it stood just over the pepper tree. Liz heard the big clock downstairs begin to strike, and she squeezed Keechie's arm. The girls leaned forward. Suddenly, a streak of light appeared in the sky and raced for the moon. The rushing light collided with the moon and there was a flash like heat lightning and Liz thought she heard a distant rumbling.

"Keechie, did you see? Did you see?"

"Sure, Lizzie," Keechie said. " 'Manda said."

Liz ran down the hall to her brother's room. She heard the chair scraping the floor. Tom was sitting in it when she entered.

"Tom, did you see?"

"See what? There isn't anything to see."

But Liz saw that the curtain in the window was still waving and she knew that Tom had been holding it aside. Tom saw her look at the curtain.

"I guess it's going to storm," he said.

Liz smiled, and went back to her room to help Keechie to bed.

"Snuggle me up, Lizzie," Keechie said.

"Good night, Keechie, dear," Liz said, still smiling happily.

2　The Feud

Liz and Keechie were playing house on their back porch. They had brought out all the dolls and all the doll clothes and the doll buggy and bathtub and the beds for the dolls. Liz had found boxes in the shed to make extra beds and had raided the linen closet for towels to use as blankets. Then, because the porch was still not completely enclosed, they had wheeled up the tricycles and the wagon to make more walls. But now that it was all arranged and their mother had not once appeared to tell them to stop making such a mess, Liz was tired of the game. She was tired of all their games, but most of all she was tired of waiting for Keechie's birthday. They had waited a long time, and the birthday was still not until tomorrow. Liz sat down sadly on the porch swing and pushed at the table with her feet to make the swing rock.

"What shall we play now, Keechie?"

"Let's play happy birthday," Keechie said at once.

"Oh, Keechie, we just did before we played house." Liz dropped her feet and didn't even bother to push the swing. She decided to go and look in the cooky jar even though she was quite sure that it was empty. As she started to get up, she heard a loud commotion coming from Amanda's yard next door. There was a thumping and a banging and the loud, deep barking of Rip, the Dunns' dog. Something exciting was about to happen. Rip was using a special bark that meant he was heading for trouble.

"Come on, Keechie," Liz said. "Rip's got a cat!"

The girls ran out of their gate and down the alley into Amanda's yard. They stopped just inside the gate, and Keechie edged up slightly behind Liz.

Billy, Amanda's brother, sat in the middle of the yard clutching Amanda's black cat while Rip danced around him, barking and growling. Wild with excitement, Rip charged into Billy. The cat clawed at Billy, jumped clear, and bounced for the top of the wall. But the wall was too high. Twisting, the cat fell back and turned to rake Rip's nose as he charged in again. The cat dodged and ran for the other side of the yard.

Liz and Keechie squealed, Billy cried, Mrs. Cook slammed out of her house screaming, "Billy!" and

Mrs. Dunn and Tom ran into the yard shouting, "Rip!" Mrs. Dunn began to beat on Rip with a magazine while Tom tried to get a grip on his collar. Rip tore loose, collided with Keechie, knocking her flat on the ground, and dashed after the cat again. Just then Amanda appeared around the corner of the house, and the cat leaped safely to her shoulder. Rip charged at Amanda and was met squarely in the face by a blast of water from the garden hose Amanda held in her hand.

"Get that dog home and tie him up!" Mrs. Dunn ordered.

Keechie picked herself up off the ground, and Mrs. Dunn went over to Billy, who was being comforted by his mother. Tom dragged Rip out the gate, and the two mothers went into Amanda's house carrying Billy between them.

Liz watched Amanda put away the hose and sit down beside her cat. She talked gently; the cat was still quivering. Liz and Keechie sat down beside her.

"A pretty good fight," Amanda said.

"Is Billy killed?" Liz asked.

"No," Amanda said. "He's scratched, though."

In a few minutes Billy came out to show them a brilliant display of colored Band-Aids. Keechie looked at them enviously and then examined her own arms and legs for scratches.

"I'm so sorry, Mrs. Cook," Mrs. Dunn said, coming out of the house. "We'll have to do something about that dog." Mrs. Cook assured her rather grimly that no great harm had been done. Mrs. Dunn patted Billy on the head, "Liz and Keechie, you come home and clean up that mess on the back porch."

Liz and Keechie followed their mother home. They found Tom comforting Rip, who was tied to a post on the porch. Tom had brought out a pan of water and was carefully washing the scratches on Rip's nose.

"I wouldn't waste any sympathy on him," Mrs. Dunn said as she went into the house. "They'll probably never speak to us again. Liz, get those bath towels back in the house."

Liz watched the door close behind her mother and then began to fold bath towels.

"Tom, do you think Amanda will speak to us again?"

"Who cares?" Tom said. "Come on, Rip, old boy, I'll take you for a walk." He led Rip out the gate.

"Keechie, do you think Amanda will speak to us?"

"Yes," Keechie said. "She will," and Keechie carefully began to wrap each of the dolls in one of the towels Liz had just folded.

Liz wandered off thoughtfully and climbed up the pepper tree to the patio wall. Amanda was still sitting in her yard talking to the cat.

"Amanda," Liz called softly. But Amanda didn't look up, and Liz was afraid to call again. She heard a scraping behind her, and Keechie appeared beside her on the wall.

" 'Manda," Keechie called loudly, "come here."

Amanda got up and walked over to them.

"What?" she asked.

"Amanda," Liz said hesitatingly, "will you speak to us?"

"Sure."

"See, Lizzie," Keechie said. "I told you."

"Why?" Amanda asked.

"Well," Liz said, "Mama said you wouldn't speak to us."

"Oh, you mean because we're having a feud? That's all right. I like feuds."

Liz was very relieved. She kicked her heels happily against the wall, and decided that she would like to get the porch straightened up.

"Move, Keechie," she said. But Keechie was staring down into Amanda's yard, watching the cat chase a grasshopper.

"I want a kitty," Keechie said.

"Um-mm," Amanda said.

"You said you would," Keechie said accusingly.

"Yes, I did," Amanda said. "I'd give you a kitty, Keechie, but you have a dog."

"I want a kitty," Keechie repeated. "And you said."

"Mama won't let you have a kitty," Liz said. "Rip would kill it."

Amanda reached into her pocket and produced three squares of bubble gum. She handed two up to the girls on the wall and unwrapped the third. She began to chew the gum methodically.

"Liz," Amanda said, "you ask your mother if Keechie could have a kitty if Rip liked the kitty and wouldn't hurt it."

"Rip doesn't like any cats," Liz said.

Amanda put her tongue in her gum and blew out,

but the gum only popped against her tongue. "I have a kitten Rip might like." She turned her back on Liz and Keechie, and wandered off toward her house. "You ask your mother, Liz," she called back. "Remember, now."

Liz didn't have much time to think about what Amanda had said. She straightened up the porch energetically, trying to keep out of her mother's way. Mrs. Dunn was angry with all of them, and by the time the family had gathered at the supper table, she was particularly angry with her husband.

"John," she began almost as soon as he had taken his seat, "you've simply got to do something about that dog. He went after the Cooks' cat again today. This time their little boy was holding the cat and he was knocked over and all scratched up and it's a miracle he wasn't hurt worse. That's the third time this week that Rip's broken into their yard after that cat."

"Ah, Mom," Tom said, "it's only a cat."

"I hate Rip," Liz declared, and she and her brother glared at each other.

"Dogs have been chasing cats for quite a few years," Mr. Dunn said calmly. "You really can't expect me to change their natures."

Mike gurgled happily from his playpen. Then he reached out for a rubber duck, lost his balance, toppled over, and began to cry. Automatically, Mrs. Dunn rose from the table and pulled him back up to a sitting position.

"It's all very well for you to be so calm about it," she continued. "You can go off to your office every day, but I have to live in this neighborhood. And the neighbors have been very decent about it. Rip knocks over their garbage cans and digs up their bushes, and nobody's complained. But he's gone too far when he starts hurting innocent children."

"Rip wouldn't hurt anybody," Mr. Dunn said. "He's a fine dog."

"I hate Rip," Liz said.

Hearing his name, Rip came around the corner of the dining room. He went over and sat down beside Liz and rested his head on her knee. Still hating him, Liz reached down and scratched his ear.

Tom rose disgustedly. "Come on, Rip," he said, and led him out into the yard.

Mrs. Dunn poured the coffee; Mr. Dunn leaned back in his chair and lighted a cigar.

"The cat will learn to stay out of Rip's way," he said.

"The cat may," Mrs. Dunn said. "But they have a litter of kittens, you know. Wait until they're old enough to come out, and Rip discovers them."

"Mama," Keechie said, "I want a kitty."

"That's all we need," Mrs. Dunn said.

"Mama," Liz began slowly, "if Rip liked a kitty and wouldn't bite it, then could we have a cat?"

"Rip doesn't," her mother said shortly.

"But, Mama"—Liz tried to explain it carefully—"what if Rip did? What if Rip would like a kitty? Then could we?"

"Why, I suppose so," her mother said. "I've nothing against cats. I'd like you to have a cat. But it's just out of the question."

Liz scraped out her bowl of chocolate pudding. "I think I'll go over to Amanda's."

"All right," her mother said. "But wash off your

mouth. And ask Mrs. Cook if I can borrow her baking soda. I've got to bake Keechie's cake and I can't find mine."

"For my happy birthday?" Keechie cried delightedly.

"Yes," her mother said, and smiled for the first time that evening. She even spoke gently to her husband. "Isn't there anything you can do, John?"

As Liz went out the door she heard her father laugh. "I'm afraid it would take a tiger to stop Rip," he said.

Amanda answered the door when Liz knocked. Liz borrowed the baking soda, and the two girls went upstairs. Amanda closed her bedroom door, and they went over to look at the kittens sleeping in their basket. Liz stroked them gently. The kittens stirred and came tumbling out of the basket. They were young and round and still a little uncertain as they skidded around on the waxed floor. There was a yellow one and a gray one and a striped one that looked just like the tiger in Keechie's book of baby animals.

"What did she say?" Amanda asked.

"She said 'yes.'"

"Then Keechie could have a cat if Rip wouldn't hurt it?"

"Yes, I told you. But Rip hates cats."

Amanda smiled, and picked up the tiny striped kitten. "I think Rip might like this cat," she said slowly. She stroked the kitten fondly. "You see, it's not a cat at all. It's a tiger."

24

"Oh," Liz gasped, and backed away from Amanda. "Mama wouldn't let Keechie have a tiger."

"She won't know," Amanda put the kitten back down on the floor.

"It looks like a kitten." Liz looked at the striped kitten carefully. It did look a little different from the other two kittens. It was just a tiny bit larger and it didn't wobble or stumble when it moved, and there was something a little scary about the way it crouched and sprang at the other kittens. "Will it grow up to be a tiger?"

"No," Amanda said. "You see, it's in disguise."

"What does that mean?"

"That means it really is a tiger," Amanda explained. "But it doesn't look like a tiger because if it did it would have to go and live at the zoo. So it's disguised as a cat."

"Would you give it to Keechie?"

"I guess I'll have to."

"It's too little," Liz said. "I think Rip would kill it." She was still not quite sure that she wanted a tiger in the family.

"No," Amanda said. "He won't try more than once."

"How do you know?"

"You'll see," Amanda touched the striped kitten lightly with one finger. "Tonight, after your mother and father go to bed, I'll call up to your window. You let Rip out. Then watch. You'll see."

Amanda seemed to consider the matter settled, and Liz hurried home with the baking soda.

"Right to bed now," her mother said. "Tomorrow is a big day, you know."

Liz intended to stay awake and wait for Amanda, but she fell asleep almost at once. It seemed she had only just gone to bed when she was awakened by a rattle against her window and a soft voice calling, "Liz." She climbed down and hurried to the window. Amanda was standing below, clearly visible in the moonlight.

"Let Rip out," Amanda called softly.

Liz went to the door and looked down the hall. The house was very dark and quiet. She thought of waking up Keechie, but Amanda hadn't said anything about that. Liz took a deep breath and started slowly down the hall. She stopped at Tom's door and whispered, "Rip."

Rip got up, shook himself, and came to the door. "Let's go outside," Liz said, and took a firm hold on Rip's collar; he led her down the stairs to the back door. Liz opened the door and let him out.

When Liz got back to her window, she could see Rip standing just beyond the porch, looking at Amanda. Amanda stood in the middle of the yard holding the tiny striped kitten. Rip saw the kitten, and bristled. Amanda turned, placed the kitten on the top of Tom's stack of boards and boxes, and backed slowly away.

A deep growl rumbled in Rip's chest. He watched the kitten eagerly. The kitten jumped down and disappeared behind the lumber pile. Rip gathered himself for action and raced after the cat. Suddenly Liz heard a snarl; her eyes opened wide; her breath caught in her throat. Over the top of the boxes came a monstrous head with huge fangs and savage eyes. With one easy spring, the beast cleared the boxes and leaped over Rip to the ground behind him. There, glaring at Rip, was the tiny kitten grown to monstrous size and ferocity. For a moment Rip stared; the cat smell was strong in the air; the hair rose on Rip's back and he charged the tiger. When Rip was only a few feet away, the tiger crouched, reached out with one paw, and struck with such force that Rip rolled back, over and over, until he was stopped by the patio wall. He got up, shook himself, and looked at the tiger in bewilderment. He was about to renew the battle when the tiger snarled and sprang. Rip whimpered and backed slowly down the wall toward the porch. The tiger sneered, and disappeared behind the pile of boxes.

Amanda looked up at Liz and raised her hand. Then she walked over to the boxes and gently stroked the tiny kitten, who sat calmly washing its face. Amanda picked up the kitten and, holding it tenderly, climbed the pepper tree and disappeared over the wall.

Liz shook her head. "Poor Rip." And even though every shadow in the dark house seemed to hide a snarling monster, she crept downstairs and let him back in the house.

By ten-thirty the next morning, the children had begun to gather for the birthday party. Keechie had insisted upon putting on her party dress the first thing in the morning, and it was already a little dirty. But Liz brushed Keechie's hair and cleaned her white shoes and she thought Keechie looked very nice. Liz had been careful to keep her own dress clean because, even though her mother kept saying it was to be a very simple party, it was, after all, Keechie's birthday party. Billy and Amanda were already there. Keechie was making sure that Billy kept his hands off the pile of presents while she sang softly, over and over, "Happy birthday to me." Liz thought Amanda looked just beautiful because Amanda was wearing her petticoat that had a row of white and a row of pink and a row of blue ruffles. The two little boys from down the alley and the girl from across the street had also arrived. They were all waiting for Tom, who had gone to get his friend Jim. Liz didn't think that her mother should have let Jim come, but Tom had said positively that he wouldn't come to a kid's party unless he could bring Jim.

Mike was out in his playpen, and Liz's mother was trying to keep the children entertained and away from the table. The table, set under the pepper tree, was gay with crepe paper and favor cups full of candy and suckers. There were hats for all the children, and balloons were tied to the chairs. On the table on the porch was a box full of prizes. Liz had helped her mother select them, and she knew that somewhere in the box was a new pair of high heels for her doll. She wondered what game she would win. She couldn't win at pin-the-tail-on-the-donkey or musical chairs, but maybe she could win the peanut race if she didn't have to race with Amanda or Tom or Jim.

Tom and Jim came in the gate, and Mrs. Dunn picked up the pile of packages and set them on the ground.

"Keechie," she said, "I think you can open your presents now."

Keechie sat down happily in front of the pile, and the other children sat around her. Tom and Jim kept an aloof distance. Keechie happily engulfed herself in papers and ribbons. As soon as she found out what was in one package, she hurried on to the next. Liz was a little shocked at her lack of interest in the cards that told who the packages came from. By the time Keechie came to the end of her packages, Liz had dressed and undressed Keechie's new doll, the two boys from down the alley were trying to play leapfrog with Keechie's ironing board, and Tom and Jim had gone off to load the water pistol Jim had given Keechie.

"That's all," Keechie announced, and was about to

get up when Amanda handed her a shoe box tied up with a big pink ribbon. Keechie untied the bow and took the lid off the box.

"A kitty!" she cried. "For me." She took the tiny striped kitten out of the box and snuggled it against her cheek; Liz put down the doll, ready to get out of the way; Mrs. Dunn gasped in horror.

"Amanda," she said, "you know we can't have a cat."

"Don't worry, Mrs. Dunn," Amanda said. "Rip won't hurt this cat."

The back door slammed, and Tom and Jim came out with Rip.

30

"Hold that dog!" Mrs. Dunn shouted, but it was too late. Rip saw the cat and started for it. Mrs. Dunn rushed to save Keechie from destruction, but the kitten leaped neatly from Keechie's arms and faced Rip squarely, arching its small back and spitting. Rip skidded to a halt three feet in front of the kitten and looked at it distrustfully. The kitten crouched, and Rip backed away. Snarling, the kitten sprang, and Rip turned and ran back to the porch where he tried to clamber through the screen door. The kitten sat down and began to wash its face.

"See, Mommie," Keechie said. "Rip didn't bite the kitty. Rip likes the kitty." She picked up the kitten and carried it to her chair.

"Now you can have both a cat and a dog, Mrs. Dunn," Amanda said. "Isn't that nice?"

Mrs. Dunn stared unbelievingly at Rip.

"Yes, Amanda," Mrs. Dunn said, and Liz wondered why her mother sounded tired so early in the morning. "Very nice. And now shall we have some cake and ice cream?"

Liz looked at the striped kitten snuggled down in Keechie's lap. Slowly Liz reached out her hand and touched the kitten. Then she stroked it lightly. The kitten began to purr.

3 The Wedding

Liz sat on the swing, moving it slowly and scuffing the dirt with her bare toes. She watched the dust well up and subside; she watched the pattern her toes made in the powdery dirt. Every now and then, she glanced cautiously at Keechie to make sure that Keechie had noticed that she was being ignored. Keechie played sulkily in the sandbox; she heaped up a pile of sand and then angrily kicked it down. Liz gave Keechie another aloof look and saw Amanda come over the patio wall. Amanda didn't look at either of them. She walked around to the back door, knocked, and studied the toes of her black shoes. Mrs. Dunn answered the door.

"My mother wants to please borrow your phone book," Amanda said. "Ours is lost."

"Of course, Amanda." Mrs. Dunn went into the house and brought back the phone book. Amanda tucked it under her arm and walked straight to the pepper tree. She was about to swing up when Keechie spoke.

"Will you play with me?"

"Busy," Amanda said, and took hold of the lowest branch.

Keechie began to throw the toys out of the sandbox, banging them against the patio wall.

"Nobody will play with me," Keechie said.

"Won't Liz play with you?" Amanda asked.

"She doesn't like me," Keechie said.

Sighing, Amanda released the branch and leaned against the tree.

"She won't ever like me." Keechie's voice trailed away in a whimper, then rose again defiantly. "I don't like you either, Lizzie."

Liz glared at her indignantly. "She lost my paper dolls," she said. "And they were brand new."

Keechie looked away and solemnly began to dig a hole in the sand.

"Keechie took them outside and lost them," Liz went on. "There was a bride and a groom and a flower girl in a pink dress and lots more. I hadn't even finished cutting them out. And now they're lost."

"Maybe Mommy will buy you some more," Keechie said.

"No, she won't." Liz was quite positive about it. "She'll say I should have put them away."

"I'm sorry, Lizzie," Keechie said. Liz and Keechie stared at each other tentatively.

"Let's have a tea party," Amanda said. "Liz, you make the tea. Keechie, you set the table and I'll bake the cakes."

"All right," Keechie said, and jumped up eagerly. She hauled a large board off Tom's lumber pile and laid it beside the sandbox. She found three coffee-can lids, three spoons, and three empty orange-juice cans among the toys she had recently hurled from the sandbox, and arranged them on the board.

Liz got up with a proper show of reluctance, picked up a bucket, and went off to fill it with water.

Amanda found a rusty muffin pan, a large bucket, and some tin cans. Carefully, she began to measure out the ingredients. "Flour," she said, "sugar, butter, baking powder." She stirred vigorously. "What kind of cake do you want, Keechie?"

"Pink," Keechie said, "and green."

"I want chocolate," Liz said, pouring her water and sand mixture into an old coffeepot. "What kind are you going to have, Amanda?"

"Mocha." Amanda spooned her mixture into the muffin cups. "Two pink and green," she said, "two chocolate, and two mocha. There." She placed the pan on the top of the patio wall. "Put the tea up here to heat, Liz," she said, "and while we wait for the cakes to bake, we'll build a castle."

They built a lovely castle in the middle of the sandbox. It was almost two feet high with a large dome on top. They mixed sand with water, and dribbled it on the castle to make turrets and towers. They put grass around the outside and decorated the bottom of the castle with pink petals from a fading rose. They made a large door with columns and took gravel from the driveway to make windows. It took a long time, and when they finished they were hot and tired and pleased.

"I smell something," Keechie said.

Liz sniffed the air. "The cakes!" she cried.

"The cakes!" Amanda said. "I forgot all about them." She jumped up and lifted the cakes down from the wall. "They're all right," she said. "Not burned at all." Amanda looked at the sand castle. "It's so hot, I think we better go inside to eat them."

"Mama won't let us take sand in the house." Liz said it softly. She didn't think that was what Amanda meant. Amanda continued to stare at the castle. It was very small, Liz thought, but how nice and cool and quiet it would be inside.

"Could we?" she asked.

"I think so," Amanda said. "If we concentrate. Keechie, can you concentrate?"

"No," Keechie said. "But I can count."

"All right," Amanda took Keechie's hand. "If you can't concentrate, you might as well count. Here, Liz, you hold the cakes." Amanda handed the muffin pan to Liz and took hold of her other hand. "Close your eyes and I'll say a poem. It helps you concentrate." Liz closed her eyes, and Amanda chanted:

> "Close your eyes
>
> And open your mouth,
>
> And point your toes,
>
> Straight to the south."

Liz concentrated hard for a long time until the muffin pan began to slip. She dropped Amanda's hand to grab the pan and opened her eyes. She was standing beside Amanda and Keechie just inside the door of a large room. The room was very high, and the light filtered down dimly from small windows set far up in the walls. Gradually her eyes became accustomed to the light and she could see that the room was filled with rows of chairs lined up on either side of a wide aisle. She heard voices and, looking down the room, saw people gathered about a large table, talking with great excitement. They looked familiar, but Liz couldn't remember where she had seen them before. One voice rose above the others.

"The preacher," the voice said. "Where's the

preacher? We can't have a wedding without the preacher."

A woman stepped out of the group around the table and peered down the room at them. "There," the woman cried excitedly and, pointing at the girls, bustled down the aisle. She was a stout woman dressed in a frilly blue dress. As she came closer, Liz saw that she wore a matching blue hat with a veil and a large corsage. She stopped and looked at them in surprise.

"Are you the preacher?" she demanded.

Liz stared curiously at the woman for a moment and then shouted, "My paper dolls!" She looked down the room at the people huddled around the table and recognized the bride and the groom and the little flower girl in the pink dress. "Keechie," she said. "It's my paper dolls. Here they are!"

The woman took off her glasses and looked down at Liz distastefully. "Where's the preacher?" she asked.

"There wasn't any," Liz said.

"What!" the woman cried furiously. "There's got to be a preacher."

"Well, there wasn't," Liz said. "Mama said I could only spend a quarter."

The woman replaced her glasses and threw up her hands in despair.

"Lunatics," she said. "Lunatics. How can you expect any cooperation from a bunch of lunatics?" Liz moved closer to Amanda. "My beautiful wedding, and now there's no preacher."

Amanda stepped forward. "I'll be the preacher."

"You will?" the woman said. "Wonderful. Let me introduce myself. I'm the bride's mother. I've been to no end of trouble and expense . . ." She stopped and looked at Amanda suspiciously. "You don't look like a preacher."

At the far end of the room the other members of the wedding party were milling about, either looking for something or trying to find out what someone else was looking for. Above this confusion, the shrill voice of the bride was raised in argument.

"I'll do very nicely for this wedding," Amanda assured her.

"You will?" the bride's mother said. "Well, all right. Come along then, come along." She seized Amanda by the arm and dragged her down the aisle. Liz took Keechie by the hand and followed slowly behind.

"Here we are, everybody," the bride's mother called. "Here's the, ah, the"—she looked down at Amanda, but Amanda held her head high and looked her straight in the eye—"the preacher," the woman finished quickly. "We're all ready to begin. Places everybody, to your places." She clapped her hands together, and the little flower girl began to cry. Liz started toward her but saw that the flower girl's beautiful dress had a great slash that ran all the way from the hem to the waist. Then Liz remembered, and decided that she didn't want to discuss that matter with the flower girl.

She returned to stand beside Keechie while everyone else darted about looking for his place.

"No, no, no, this won't do at all," the bride's mother said. "You two," she pointed at the groom and the best man, "stand over there."

"What?" The groom cupped his hand beside his head. "What, where?" he called.

"What's the matter with the man!" the bride's mother said, stamping her foot. Amanda stepped up and led the groom and the best man to their places on the right of the table. The bride's mother picked up the cushion bearing the ring and looked around distractedly. "The ring bearer," she said. "Where's the ring bearer?"

"I didn't have time to cut him out," Liz said.

"What!" the bride's mother shrieked. "You didn't cut him out? I never heard of such thoughtlessness."

"Well, you were all just brand new," Liz said. "And Keechie lost you before I had time."

Keechie glared at Liz.

Keechie can be the ring bearer," Amanda said. Keechie smiled, but the bride's mother continued to scowl. She looked at Keechie dubiously.

"I don't think she'll do. She's not a boy, and even if she were she doesn't look the least bit reliable."

Amanda sighed wearily, and Liz saw the bride's father, who had been standing unobtrusively on the outskirts of the group, edge over to his wife. He patted her arm.

40

"There, there, dear," he said. "I'm sure it will be all right." He glanced at his watch. "I have a very important meeting at four o'clock and we'd better get started. Perhaps she'll pretend she's a boy."

"No, I won't," Keechie said.

"You see"—the bride's mother pointed at Keechie accusingly—"not the least bit reliable." But Amanda stepped up and took the cushion and ring away from the bride's mother and handed it to Keechie. Keechie smiled admiringly at the ring and went to stand beside the groom.

"Good, good," the bride's father said. "Could we get started now?"

The bride looked at him aghast. "But I have to walk up the aisle," she said.

The bride's father glanced at his watch again. "Oh, very well," he said. "If you must. Perhaps you could run."

"Father!" The bride was shocked.

"There, there, dear," her father said. "Just a little joke. Come along." He began to lead her down the aisle to the door. "Come along," he called to the bridesmaid, who had not left the table.

"I can't," she said. The bridesmaid had been trying to set a large vase of flowers on the table. "When I let go of the vase, it tips over." Liz looked at the vase in alarm; the bottom of it was very wavy. It really wasn't her fault, Liz thought Her mother had refused to let her use the good scissors.

"You have to come," the bride's mother said, and pulled the bridesmaid away from the table. The vase fell with a crash, and the flowers spilled all over the table.

"You see," the bridesmaid wailed.

"There, there," the bride's father said. "I think it looks very nice that way." He conducted the bride, the mother, the bridesmaid, and the flower girl down the aisle to the door.

"First me," the bride's mother called. "First the usher has to seat me."

"There wasn't any usher," Liz said, but Amanda held her finger up to her lips.

"You go and be the usher, Liz," Amanda whispered.

Liz didn't like the idea much but she obeyed and put the cakes down on the chair beside her and walked over to the bride's mother. The bride's mother placed her hand on Liz's arm and marched up the aisle to her place in the front row of chairs. .

"Now the other guests," she said.

"There aren't any other guests," Liz said.

"Nonsense! I want you to know, young lady, that I have a great many friends who would most certainly not disappoint me on such an occasion."

Liz looked at Amanda. Amanda winked and waved her back down the aisle. Feeling very foolish, Liz made several solitary trips up and down the aisle. When Amanda thought a sufficient number of guests had been seated, she nodded at Liz and beckoned to the flower girl. The flower girl hurried up the aisle, nervously clutching the slash in her dress. She quickly reached her place, and the bridesmaid started up the aisle. She advanced with dignity until she reached the table with the overturned flowers. She pounced upon them, gathering and stuffing the flowers back into the lopsided vase. Next came the bride. Leaning heavily upon her father's arm, she limped up the aisle. They were almost halfway when the bride's mother jumped up.

"Wait," she said. "The music. We've got to have music. Where's the organist?"

"There wasn't any," Liz said.

The bride's mother looked at her unbelievingly. "Whoever heard of a wedding without music?"

"Could you sing, Liz?" Amanda asked.

"I can't sing very well."

"She certainly doesn't look like she could sing," the bride's mother said.

"But I'll try," Liz went on, and began to sing loudly:

> "Here comes the bride
> All dressed in white.
> See how she wiggles
> From side to side."

The bride, who had continued to limp up the aisle, stopped suddenly.

"Wiggles!" she said. "Wiggles! It's wobbles. How

dare you insult a poor cripple? Can I help it if my leg was cut off and put back crooked with Scotch Tape?"

"Well," Liz said. "I couldn't help it either. The Scotch Tape got twisted and it wouldn't stick on right."

"Oh," the bride whimpered, and seemed about to collapse; but her father patted her arm and continued to lead her up the aisle. "There, there, dear," he said. "Wiggles, wobbles, what does it matter?" Liz, feeling quite insulted, stopped her singing, and the bride and her father reached their places in silence.

Amanda faced them all solemnly; she coughed twice behind her hand, took a large book out of the pocket of her skirt, opened it in the middle and began to read: " 'Quade, Henry, 1031 Venice Ave., EA 7-2261; Quail, T. J., 4607 S. 12th St., MA 3-2746; Quakenbush, Rudy, 2070 Pennsylvania Dr., MA 2-7078.' " The bride's mother showed signs of doubt as Amanda continued to read; she fidgeted nervously and waved her arms about. By the time Amanda reached " 'Quality Cleaners, 5522 Rosewood Ave., EA 7-9809,' " the bride's mother had jumped to her feet.

"Are you sure you have the right book?"

"Silence," Amanda commanded. She looked at the bride's mother severely. "If there are any more interruptions, we shall have to clear the court." Firmly, Amanda closed the book and placed it on the table. She turned to the bride.

"Do you take this man to be your lawfully wedded husband?"

44

The bride blushed prettily. "I do," she said.

Amanda turned to the groom. "Do you take this woman to be your lawfully wedded wife?"

"What, what, where?" The groom looked about in confusion.

Amanda repeated the question.

"What?" the groom said again. "Could you speak a little louder? I don't hear very well."

"Keechie cut off his ears," Liz said.

"No ears!" the bride shrieked, and appeared about to faint.

"He does," Amanda said, and beckoned Keechie and the best man forward. "With this ring . . ." Amanda held out her hand for the ring.

"The ring," called the best man. "Where's the ring?" They all stared at the pillow Keechie held in her hands. It was empty.

"I told you she wasn't reliable," the bride's mother said.

Amanda looked sternly at Keechie. "Keechie," she said, "where is the ring?" Keechie dropped her eyes and reached up into her pocket. Reluctantly she brought out the ring and gave it to the best man.

"Thief," the bride's mother called.

The ring passed from hand to hand until it was safely on the bride's finger.

"I pronounce you man and wife," Amanda said solemnly.

The bride's mother cried loudly; the flower girl cried

softly. The groom shouted, "What, what, where?" the best man made loud jokes about kissing the bride, and the bride's father studied his watch and wondered aloud if he could still make his meeting. Only the bride was unperturbed.

"Where's the champagne?" she said. "Where are the refreshments?" She spied the tin of cakes that Liz had set on a chair, and headed for them. "Ah," she said, "here they are." The bride caught up the muffin tin, seized one of the pink-and-green cakes and stuffed it into her mouth.

"That's mine!" Keechie shouted. The bride prepared to eat another, and Amanda hurried over.

"Wouldn't you like one of these?" she asked, pointing to the other cakes. "They're very good . . . mocha and chocolate."

"No, I want this one," the bride said, and removed the second pink-and-green cake. "It's my wedding."

"It's my cake," Keechie said, and threw her pillow at the bride. The bride, hit right in the face, cried out and dropped the cake. Keechie grabbed it and darted out of the way just as the bride threw the muffin pan. The pan missed Keechie and bounced off the wall.

The bride jumped up and down while her mother cried, "Thief, thief," and heaved the telephone book. Keechie ducked behind Liz, and the book banged against the wall. The bridesmaid joined in and happily hurled her vase of flowers. Liz felt bits of sand

46

dropping on her head. A crack had opened up in the wall.

"The castle's caving in!" Amanda called. "Run for your lives!" She seized Keechie with one hand and Liz with the other and the three girls raced down the aisle. They flung the door open and jumped out just as the sand house collapsed behind them.

Panting, Liz and Amanda sat down beside the sandbox. Keechie began to cry. The back door opened, and Mrs. Dunn walked over. She stooped down beside her daughter.

"What's the matter, dear?" she asked. She looked at the girls and at the ruined sand castle. "Oh," she said, "did your house fall in? Never mind, dear. Maybe Liz and Amanda will help you build another."

"No," Keechie wailed. "I don't want another."

"I know, dear." Mrs. Dunn patted Keechie comfortingly. "Another is never quite so nice, is it? But maybe you can build an even bigger one."

"No." Keechie cried more loudly.

"Liz, have you been fighting with Keechie?" Mrs. Dunn asked severely.

"No, Mommy."

"Look, if you're still fretting about those paper dolls, I'll get you another set."

"Oh, no, Mommy," Liz said. "I don't want another set." Liz looked as if she too were about to cry.

"What's the matter with them, Amanda?"

"Maybe an ant bit Keechie," Amanda said.

Mrs. Dunn sighed, and shook her head. She picked up Keechie. "Come along, dear. We'll go inside and get a nice cool drink and I'll sing you a song."

Keechie put her head on her mother's shoulder and allowed herself to be carried off. As they disappeared into the house, Liz saw the remains of a pink-and-green cake clutched in Keechie's hand.

4   The Flying Red Horse

"Amanda," Liz said, "you told my mama a lie." This had been clear to Liz as soon as Amanda, holding Keechie by the hand, had led them down the walk, turned the wrong way, and walked briskly off in the wrong direction. Liz glanced back nervously at her house. "You told my mama that we were going to your house."

"Well, we're not," Amanda said.

"Where are we going?"

"To the stores." Amanda walked on.

Liz scrooched down behind the privet hedge. Along her block of West Jefferson, the hedges were almost all the same height. When Liz stood on tiptoe, she could see over the hedge into the yard behind it; when she scrooched down just a little, she was completely hidden from view. She kept close behind Keechie. Keechie was too little to be seen even from the windows in the second floor of their house, but Amanda could be seen clearly from any of them. Liz shivered, she could almost feel the impact of the voice that would summon her home.

But the late afternoon silence was not broken. They reached the corner, turned it, and Liz felt safely beyond the range of her mother's eye. Amanda walked a little faster, and Liz ran to catch up.

"But you know," Liz said, "Mama would never, never let us take Keechie so far."

"Of course not. That's why I told her we were going to my house."

"Oh." Liz hesitated, but only for a moment. Her moral instincts were strong. "It's not nice to tell lies," she said.

"Well, it's not nice to hurt people's feelings, either, is it? If your mama knew we'd taken Keechie so far she'd have to punish you, wouldn't she? Think how bad that would make her feel."

Liz thought about it and decided that Amanda was probably right. They came to the next corner, and Amanda stopped and looked back.

"Go and get Keechie," she said.

Keechie had halted a quarter of a block behind them. She was squatting with her nose two inches above the sidewalk.

"Ladybuggie," Keechie called. "Come see."

Liz walked back and squatted beside her.

"Oh, it is not," Liz said. "It's just an old beetle."

Amanda, angry and impatient, arrived beside them. "June bug," she pronounced decisively. "Come along. We've got a lot to do and we'll never get there if we have to stop and look at every bug along the way." Keechie spotted a cat ahead and trotted off beside Amanda. Liz followed a little resentfully. She was practically certain that it couldn't be a June bug because Keechie's birthday was in June and that was a long time ago. Liz sulked along behind until she saw that Amanda and Keechie had reached the corner. Then she hurried up to them. Liz was old enough to cross streets by herself, but she had to watch out for Keechie.

"What are we going to do, Amanda?" Liz asked.

"Get the flying red horse."

Liz gasped, "Oh, Amanda. Can we?"

"We'll have to," Amanda said. "Tomorrow is Billy's birthday. He wants a rocking horse, and Mother won't get him one. He's going to be three, and Mother says that's too big for rocking horses. But that's what Billy wants, so we'll just have to get it."

"How can we get it, Amanda?" Liz persisted.

"If you'd stop asking so many silly questions, I could think about it."

Liz followed Amanda in respectful silence. A small boy threw a handful of pebbles at them; Amanda ignored him. A large dog came out to bark at them;

Amanda said, "Scat," and the dog obeyed. They reached the corner opposite the shopping center.

"Keechie, come and take my hand and don't step off the curb," Amanda said.

Across the street, the stores stretched in a long line from the corner gas station to the laundromat at the other end. Liz did not see them; she looked only at the pole rising in front of the gas station. There he was, the marvelous creature, just above the sign that said "Mobilgas." The horse, brilliantly poised, with his wings outstretched, was ready for flight. His redness glittered in the sun. Liz stared upward.

"Amanda, isn't he beautiful?" she whispered.

"Green light, go," Keechie said. The three girls walked slowly across the street and stood in a circle underneath the horse, gazing up at him.

"He isn't ours, Amanda," Liz said. "We can't just take him. That would be stealing."

"Maybe they'll give him to us." Amanda looked around the gas station.

One man was putting gas into a car, another was inside the building, and a third was outside the garage, taking a tire off a rim.

"Keechie," Amanda said, "see the man with the big tire? Go and ask him to give you the horse."

Keechie shook her head. Amanda stooped beside her, one arm around Keechie, the other pointing up at the horse. Her voice coaxed. "See the pretty horsie,

Keechie. I need him. Go and ask the nice man to give him to us."

"No," Keechie said.

Amanda stood up and reached into the pocket of her skirt. She produced a square of bubble gum. "Want some bubble gum, Keechie?"

Keechie nodded and held out her hand. Amanda withdrew the gum, keeping it in sight but out of reach.

"I want some bubble gum," Keechie said.

"After you ask the man," Amanda said. "I'll give it to you as soon as you come back. Just go up to him and say, 'May I have the horse?' "

Keechie looked at Amanda doubtfully, and turned and walked toward the man with the tire. She approached him from the rear and stopped behind him. Liz and Amanda went to the water fountain a few feet away and took turns letting the icy water gurgle against their mouths. Keechie began to circle the man. She went around him twice, without ever crossing his line of vision. The man looked up and watched her as she circled warily for a third time.

"Hello." He smiled.

"May I have the horse?" Keechie said.

"What?"

"May I have the horsie?" Keechie pointed at the Mobilgas sign and the horse above it.

"You want that horse?" The man was astonished.

" 'Manda needs it," Keechie's voice quavered.

"You want that horse." The man threw back his head, and laughed. "Sure," he said, "sure, little girl. Help yourself."

Keechie turned and fled to Amanda and Liz. The man watched them as they hastily drew her away. He laughed again and returned to his work.

"You see," Amanda said as she gave Keechie the bubble gum. Amanda found two more pieces of bubble gum in her pocket. The girls chewed thoughtfully and walked back past the horse to the corner where a bench marked the bus stop. They sat on it backward, their legs dangling, and watched the horse. Liz rested her chin on the back of the bench, and sighed. They had been given the horse, but he looked just as unattainable as ever.

"He's ours, Amanda?" she said hopefully. Amanda didn't answer and Liz didn't dare speak again. But when she looked at Amanda, she was encouraged. Amanda was blowing the largest bubble Liz had ever seen. Ordinarily Amanda did not blow bubbles, but sometimes when she was planning something she forgot. If the plan was a good one she went right on blowing until the bubble popped and the gum got smeared on her face. As Liz watched, the bubble burst. Amanda wearily took the gum out of her mouth, rolled it into a ball, and dabbed the gum from her face. Liz smiled.

"We'll need a ladder," Amanda said, "and a rope or something to use for reins." She threw her gum away. "Well, there's no point in sitting here. Come on, Keechie." Amanda led them across the parking lot. They passed the drugstore and the hardware store, paused to look at the shoes in the shoe store, and stopped in front of the grocery. They arrived just as a red-faced clerk came out dragging a small black-and-white dog. He released the dog and went back into the store. After two resentful barks, the dog sat down to wait by the door. Amanda squeezed Liz's arm.

"Come on," she said. With careful indifference,

Amanda held the door open for Liz and Keechie and the small black-and-white dog. The dog barked furiously and immediately disappeared down one of the aisles. The girls studied the gum in the gum machine while they waited. They did not wait for long. The clerk, angrier and redder than before, soon appeared dragging the dog along by the collar; he hustled him outside. Amanda winked slyly at Liz. Liz tried to wink back but blinked both eyes instead. Amanda had already started back through the store. Liz coaxed Keechie away from the showcase of chocolate-covered doughnuts, and they followed Amanda out the side door and back around the store. When they arrived at the front door, the dog was waiting. Amanda held the door open again while Liz, Keechie, and the dog reentered. This time the girls hurried after the dog until they caught up with him barking and sniffing happily among the vegetables.

"Let's pat the nice doggie, Keechie," Amanda said.

She grasped the dog by the collar while Keechie bent over him crooning, "Nice doggie, nice doggie." The dog barked and wriggled happily.

"Here he comes," Liz whispered. The red-faced clerk came down the aisle.

"Is this your dog?'" he demanded. "We don't allow dogs in here."

"He keeps following us in," Amanda said apologetically.

"Can't one of you hold him outside?"

Amanda looked at Liz and Keechie. "They're too little." Liz choked back her outrage. "I could tie him up," Amanda went on, "if I had something to tie him up with. But I don't." She looked up at the clerk.

"Oh, all right," he said. "I'll get you something. Wait here and hang onto him." The clerk was back in a few minutes with a length of rope. "Here," he said. "Now, don't let him in again."

Amanda looped the rope through the dog's collar. "Come on," she said. Amanda dragged on the dog, Liz dragged on Keechie, and they ran out of the store. They went all the way down the row of stores, past the clothing store, past the dime store, where they stopped for a minute to look at a window full of swim rings and flippers and snorkels and wading pools, on past the laundry until they came to the wall that marked the end of the shopping center. Amanda removed the rope from the dog's collar.

"Now scat," she said to the dog. "Go home." The dog trotted off obligingly. Liz and Amanda leaned against the wall to think. Amanda carefully began to coil the rope into a neat loop.

"Here's the rope," she said. "But where will we get the ladder?" Liz looked about hopefully, but there was no ladder in sight and Keechie was gone too.

"Where's Keechie?" she asked.

"Just right up here." Keechie's voice floated down

to them casually. They turned. She was standing on top of the wall.

"What are you doing up there?" Amanda demanded.

"Just looking at the tractor."

Amanda stood on tiptoe and looked over the wall. " 'Lou's Rental Equipment. Why buy it when you can rent it?' " Amanda read. "They'd have a ladder," she said.

"It wouldn't work," Liz said.

Amanda looked at her. "Why not?"

"Daddy got a lawn mower there. It wouldn't go."

"Oh, well, ladders are different," Amanda said. "They don't have to go. Come on, Keechie."

The three girls scrambled over the wall. They inspected the trailers and the power mowers and the wheelbarrows outside Lou's Rental Equipment, and then went in. A very fat man stood behind the counter shuffling through a pile of pink tickets. He paid no attention to them. Amanda walked straight to the counter.

"Do you have a ladder?" she asked.

Without much interest, the man looked them over. "What would you want with a ladder?"

"It's my kitten," Amanda explained. "It climbed up the pepper tree and now it can't get down."

"You'd better wait until your daddy comes home. He'll get it down."

"He is home," Amanda said. "He's up the pepper tree too."

"Your daddy's up the pepper tree too?" The man became a little more interested.

"He climbed up to get the kitten and the branch broke and now we need a ladder."

The man looked confused. "Maybe you'd better wait until your mother . . ."

"She's gone to borrow a station wagon to bring home the ladder," Amanda said. "She said we were to come and rent the ladder and have it all ready when she got here with the car."

The man blinked his eyes and shook his head. Liz had backed away to watch the discussion from a safe distance. Keechie stood beside her, investigating the tools on the table in front of them. The hammer she was holding suddenly slipped through her fingers and fell with a soft thud on her foot. Keechie let out a wail.

"There, there, honey," Amanda said quickly "We'll get your kitten. You see," she turned to the man, "we have to hurry. Daddy's very angry. He says if we don't get him down from that tree, he'll take the cat and all the kittens to the pound and that will be the end of them."

Keechie continued to cry, and the man began to weaken. "Well," he said, "come on outside. I suppose I could get it out. You're sure your mother's coming?"

Amanda nodded and they followed the man outside. "How big a ladder do you need?" he asked.

Amanda looked perplexed. Then she pointed to the Mobilgas sign. "See the sign down there," she said, "with the horse on top? That's how high Daddy is."

The man went back into the yard behind the store and returned carrying the ladder. "We'll leave it here until your mother comes."

Amanda looked at the ladder. "That's not high enough."

"You said as high as that Mobilgas sign."

"Yes," Amanda said, "and that's not high enough."

"It's plenty long," the man said. "You can take my word for it."

Amanda shook her head determinedly. "Is it Liz?"

Liz looked at the ladder. "It won't work."

"What?" the man said.

"Daddy rented a lawn mower here," Liz said, "and it wouldn't go."

The man began to perspire a little. "He probably didn't know how to work it," he said, and muttered, "Anyone who can't get down out of a tree . . . This ladder is plenty . . ." He looked at Amanda. "Hey, what are you doing?"

Amanda had picked up one end of the ladder and was dragging if off in the direction of the gas station. "Well," she said, "if you're going to be so stubborn, I'll just have to show you." She continued to pull on the ladder. The man stamped his foot in exasperation, and Keechie began to cry again.

"It won't work," Liz said.

"All right, all right," the man shouted, and picked

up the other end of the ladder. "But if I were your father, I'd stay up in that pepper tree." With Amanda at the front end and the man at the rear, they carried the ladder down the street to the gas station. When they reached the sign, the man brushed them all aside.

"Now just let me do this." He picked up the ladder and leaned it up against the sign. The ladder reached the horse handily. The man stood back with his hands on his hips and looked at it. "There," he said. "Now does it reach or doesn't it?" He looked down at Amanda, waiting for an apology, but she showed no signs of remorse. She pointed up the street to where a station wagon had stopped in front of Lou's Rental.

"My Mother," she explained. "I'll watch the ladder. You go tell her to pick us up here.

"Okay," the man said, "and the next time you want to rent something, you go to A-1 Rents, will you?" They watched him trot off down the street.

"Up you go, Keechie," Amanda said. "Hurry. Then you, Liz." Keechie was given no time to consider. Liz pulled her to the ladder and started her up. Liz stayed one step behind Keechie, pushing her gently from time to time. But Keechie needed no urging; she climbed steadily, chanting as she went, "Climbing up the ladder, climbing up the ladder." Amanda followed them, whistling cheerfully. Keechie reached the horse and climbed onto his back.

"Sit still, Keechie." Liz sat down gingerly. Amanda

passed the rope around the horse's neck and climbed on behind Liz. Keechie bounced a little; Amanda gave the reins a tentative shake or two; and Liz put her arms tightly around Keechie's waist.

"How do you suppose we make him go?" Amanda said.

"Mama always puts a dime in the slot," Liz said. "Then the horse in the store gallops."

"I don't have a dime. Do you?"

"No. Maybe Keechie has something. She always has things in her pocket. Mama won't give her a dime because she loses them but she gives her pennies. Keechie cries if she doesn't."

"Keechie, what do you have in your pocket?" Amanda asked.

Keechie investigated the pocket of her shirt. First she produced a bobby pin and showed it to Liz and Amanda. They shook their heads. Keechie looked again and brought out the nipple for a doll's bottle.

"Don't you have a penny, Keechie?" Liz asked.

Keechie peered deep into her pocket.

"I have a button," she said, bringing it out reluctantly.

"Oh, no." Amanda shook her head.

"It's red," Keechie said.

"Well, we might as well try it," Amanda said. "Put it in the horsie, Keechie." Keechie looked regretfully at her red button and then stood up and leaned out over the horse's neck.

As Liz called, "Watch out," and grabbed for Keechie's legs, she heard a faint click. Deep inside the horse, a humming began. Amanda took firm hold on the reins. The humming increased to a roar. They felt a faint stir in the wings, and then a firmer push, until suddenly the wings were beating strongly and the horse was rising. Liz closed her eyes and held on tight to Keechie. She felt them going up and up. When she opened her eyes, she knew they must be higher than the Ferris wheel.

"Don't be scared, honey," she whispered to Keechie. Keechie turned around and smiled at her.

"We're higher than your bunk bed, Lizzie." Keechie laughed.

"And don't wiggle," Liz added. She looked down. Everything was strange and unfamiliar.

"Are we in China, Amanda?" It was the farthest-away place she knew.

"No," Amanda scoffed. "Look. There's your house." Liz looked down, but all she saw were tiny boxes like the houses on her pegboard. Amanda pulled on the rope in her right hand, and the horse turned slowly and circled to the right. "There's the park," she said.

They flew twice around the park, and then Amanda pulled on the rope in her left hand and they flew twice around a gray square with green dots and brown dots like one of Keechie's paintings.

"That's the school," Amanda said.

"That's the school, Keechie," Liz said.

63

"When I get bigger, I'll go to school," Keechie said.

"Amanda," Liz said, "I think . . . I think he's just beautiful." And for a moment Liz thought she loved the horse more than anything in the world.

"I guess Billy will like him, all right," Amanda said, and she turned the horse and headed back toward their neighborhood.

"Will you take Billy flying on him, Amanda?" Liz asked.

"Oh, no. He's only going to be three. He'd fall off or something."

"Keechie's only three," Liz said.

"Yes," Amanda said, "but Billy's a boy."

They circled closer and closer in on their houses, dropping down until the horse was skimming over the patio walls. Liz began to recognize the objects on the ground. The tiny red square was her wagon, and the pink-and-blue checkerboard with one checker was Mike in his playpen.

"I guess we'd better land." Amanda pulled back on the rope. "It's probably time for supper."

"Amanda," Liz said, "be sure you don't land in my yard."

"I know what I'm doing," Amanda said crossly.

"Mama would be so angry if she knew we took Keechie to the store," Liz said.

Gently the horse landed them between the wall and the row of overgrown oleanders in Amanda's yard. The girls slid off and walked solemnly to the horse's head and patted him once lightly on the nose. The horse accepted each caress, and his wings became very still. He seemed to sigh as he settled to the ground.

5   The Time Machine

Liz sat on the floor of her room with a large sheet of paper before her and crayons scattered all about. She was making a horse but she couldn't remember whether a horse's tail went up or down, and there was no one around to ask. She decided to leave the tail out and went on to draw herself on the horse's back. She looked at the picture critically and then drew Keechie behind her on the horse's back. It was very silly, Liz thought, of Keechie to get mad and go away just because she had said that Keechie scribbled.

"She does scribble," Liz muttered, and looked up as Keechie came running up the stairs and into the room.

"Lizzie," Keechie said, "come see. Tom's made something."

"What's he made?"

"I don't know. Something. It's 'normous."

Liz glanced at her picture once and then got up and followed Keechie downstairs and outside. There beside the patio wall was the something Tom had made. It looked like a huge multicolored umbrella turned upside down.

"What is it, Lizzie?" Keechie asked.

Liz walked a little nearer. "A tent, I guess. Maybe Tom's going to have a circus."

The two girls edged forward. Liz knew that Tom did not like them fooling around anything he had made and that if he saw them he would be sure to say something insulting. But Tom was not in sight. Liz and Keechie walked slowly around Tom's creation. It was shaped with chicken wire on a wooden frame. Tom had covered the chicken wire with a blanket they used for making tents, two rugs Liz's mother had thrown out, several old bath towels, and a torn sheet. The construction was a little higher than Liz, and large enough to hold Keechie, Liz, and Rip with a little room to spare. On their second trip around, Liz and Keechie stopped in front of a place where a large green towel seemed to be hanging freely. Liz touched it cautiously and then pulled it aside.

"It's the door," Keechie said, and stuck her head in the opening.

"Hey, get out of there!" Tom yelled and came

toward them. The two girls scampered away. Tom solemnly drew the towel aside and went in, letting the green door fall behind him. Liz and Keechie exchanged a glance, and step by step came nearer.

"Tom," Liz said, "Tom, what is it?" There was no answer.

"Tommy," Keechie called winsomely, "may we come in?" Still Tom remained silent.

"Tom," Liz said, "I still have half my candy bar. You can have it."

"All right," Tom agreed. "Go get it."

"Go get it, Keechie," Liz ordered, and Keechie raced to the house and was back in a minute with the remains of a Hershey bar.

"Here." Liz took the candy from Keechie.

Tom appeared in the doorway. "You call that half?" he said, and took the candy. He drew back the green towel to reveal the inside of his building. "You can stand here and watch but don't come in. It's dangerous."

Tom returned to his work. Liz saw that he had placed a couple of boxes inside to use as tables. One of them held a can of black paint and a can of red paint. Tom was busy painting circles that looked like the faces of clocks on the sheet that covered part of one wall.

"That's nice, Tom," Liz said.

"Is it a tent?" Keechie asked. "Are you going to have a circus?"

"Naw." Tom painted two more circles. Then he reached over and twirled the steering wheel that hung from the wall oposite the door. "It's a time machine."

"Oh," Liz and Keechie said together. They stepped back from the door and collided with Amanda.

"That's dangerous," Keechie said.

"You bet," Tom said.

"What's a time machine, Tom?" Keechie asked.

"It takes you back in time," Tom said. "To any-where you want to go. You can go back as far as you want—to when there were pirates sailing the Barbary Coast or to when there were dinosaurs and cave men and stuff like that."

"Oh, I wouldn't want to go there," Liz said.

"You just get in," Tom said, "and set the machinery and you can go anywhere, back to any of the things that happened a long time ago."

"To my happy birthday, Tom?" Keechie said.

Amanda, who had remained silent, suddenly began to laugh. Liz wished she wouldn't do that because it was sure to make Tom mad. "In that thing?" Amanda said. "You'd need a strong wind behind you, and a strong wind would knock it over."

Tom ignored her. "It's not quite finished. But when it is I'm going to sail around the Cape on a sailing ship."

"Can I go, Tommy?" Keechie asked.

"Naw. Girls can't go." He stood up and looked at Amanda. "Girls can't do anything but play with dolls."

"Tom, Tom," a loud voice called. Tom's friend Jim stuck his head in at the gate. "Let's go, Tom."

"Okay." Tom dropped the green towel over the entrance and came out of the time machine. He got his bike and wheeled it toward the gate.

"Don't touch it," Tom threatened. "Don't even go near it."

"That silly contraption." Amanda tossed her head. "Who'd want to go near it?"

"You better not," Tom muttered. The girls stood listening to the sounds of Tom and Jim departing. When all was quiet, Amanda said, "Come on."

"We better not, Amanda," Liz said. "Tom gets so mad."

"He's gone," Amanda said, and the three girls squeezed into the time machine. It was not quite high enough for Amanda to stand up straight. She gave the steering wheel a spin, carefully inspected all the dials, and, picking up the paint can Tom had left open on the ground, added one more dial to the sheet. Next she examined the equipment that Tom had set out on a box. There was a broken alarm clock and Tom's boy scout compass; there was the desk lamp Liz's father had thrown out because he couldn't stand fluorescent light; and there was a canteen, and a box of crackers, and two cap pistols with two rolls of caps.

"Where shall we go?" Amanda asked.

"Oh," Liz said, "Tom wouldn't want us to go anywhere."

"He'll never know."

"Well," Liz said, "Mama wouldn't want us to go very far."

"Okay. We'll just go back to frontier days, when there were Indians and pioneers and buffaloes and bears."

"Wild Indians?"

"Yes," Amanda said, and Liz began to move toward the door. "What's the matter?" Amanda asked. "Don't you want to go?"

"I think I won't," Liz said.

"Do you want to go, Keechie?" Amanda asked.

"Yes," Keechie laughed, and started for the door.

"Then where are you going?"

71

"Just to get my Indian hat. I'll be right straight back."

While Keechie was gone, Amanda made arrangements. She set the alarm clock, studied the compass, and carefully adjusted the steering wheel. By the time she had finished, Keechie was back wearing an Indian feather bonnet and carrying her striped kitten.

"My kitty wants to go."

"Okay," Amanda said. "We're all set." She turned to Liz. "Well, are you coming or not?"

Liz stared glumly at the ground. She certainly didn't care to meet any wild Indians. She was more afraid of them than she was of Tom. But she couldn't let Keechie and Amanda go off without her.

"Yes," she said. "I'll go." She kicked the ground with her toe.

"Then turn it on," Amanda ordered.

"Turn what on?" Liz looked around, and Amanda pointed to the desk lamp. Liz pushed the switch, and a soft blue light began to fill the time machine. The light increased in brightness until everything glowed a vivid blue. Liz looked at Amanda, grimly holding the steering wheel. Her dress was blue, her hair was blue. Liz looked at Keechie; her blue eyes sparkled out of a blue face. Even Keechie's kitten had turned blue. The light reached a brilliant intensity and then began to fade. Gradually it died away and flickered out.

"Here we are," Amanda said. She picked up the

canteen and put it over her shoulder. She put the box of crackers in one pocket and the compass in the other.

"You wear these," she said, and handed the holster with the guns to Liz.

"Let's go," Amanda said and led the way out of the time machine. Keechie, still holding her kitten, followed. Liz sighed, and strapped on the guns.

The girls stopped just outside the door and looked around. The pepper tree was gone and so were the patio wall and all the houses. The country was rough and uneven, and a low line of hills blocked their view to the east. For as far as they could see, there was not a road or a car or a person. Liz was sure they were lost.

"Where are the Indians?" Keechie asked.

"I guess Tom's old machine doesn't work," Liz said hopefully.

"Let's climb up on those hills," Amanda said. "Then we can see more."

The hills rose gradually in front of them. Amanda got to the top first and stood staring at a point below.

"Look!" she cried triumphantly when Liz and Keechie had caught up to her. Liz looked where Amanda pointed, and saw a line of objects moving toward them. She was a little relieved. If they were lost, at least they were not lost alone. But as the objects moved closer, the shapes were still strange and unfamiliar.

"What is it?" Liz asked in alarm.

"A wagon train," Amanda said, and then as Liz stared she could see the horses, some carrying men and others pulling wagons with white tops. Keechie sat down and began to take off her shoes.

"They'll all be shooted," Keechie said.

"What!" Liz said.

"They'll all be shooted by the Indians."

"What Indians, Keechie?" Amanda looked around.

Keechie carefully tucked her socks into her shoes. "Why, those Indians just right over there." Keechie pointed to the line of hills across the pass. At first Liz couldn't see anything. Then something moved.

"Take cover," Amanda whispered, and fell to the ground behind a big rock. Liz ran over and crouched beside her.

"Do you see them?" Liz asked. She peered out from behind the rock at the brown shapes of the Indians on the opposite hill. But the Indians, hidden from the view of the wagon train, paid no attention to the girls.

"Keechie's right," Amanda said. "They're going to ambush the wagon train. We'll have to do something."

"Why don't we go home?" Liz looked at the Indians, and shivered. She could see the paint that striped their faces and the feathers in their hair.

"Let's sneak up on them," Keechie said.

"We'll have to warn the wagon train," Amanda said. "Before it gets here." Amanda began to creep down the hill, darting from one rock to another. She

74

turned and beckoned to Liz to follow her. Reluctantly Liz rose from behind the rock and ran after Amanda.

"Come on, Keechie," she said. Keechie picked up her shoes and her kitten and walked calmly down after Liz and Amanda.

"Hurry," Amanda called.

"Watch out, Keechie," Liz said. "The Indians will see you."

Amanda stopped at the bottom of the hill, and waited. It was open country from the hill to the wagon train.

"We'll have to run for it," Amanda said. "Maybe the Indians only have bows and arrows. Are you ready?"

"I've got a sticker," Keechie said, and sat down to examine the bottom of her foot.

Liz glared at her. "Why can't you keep your shoes on?" She sat down beside Keechie and pulled out the sticker. Then she put Keechie's shoes and socks back on. "Mama says you're to keep your shoes on so that you won't catch cold."

Keechie frowned. "I won't," she said, and reached down to pull her shoes off. An arrow bounced off the rock beside them and fell at their feet.

Liz looked indignantly toward the Indians. "They ought to be more careful."

"Can you run very, very fast, Keechie?" Amanda asked.

"Oh, yes," Keechie said.

"Let's run, then." Amanda started off toward the wagon train. Liz grabbed Keechie by the hand. Keechie stumbled and slipped, but Liz pulled her along until they caught up with Amanda. She had stopped and was watching the wagon train. The men who rode in front of the wagons were staring at the girls. One of the men held up his hand, and the wagons stopped. Another man kicked his horse and galloped toward them. He stopped a short distance away and, holding his rifle ready, stared at them in astonishment.

The girls ran to him.

"Indians," Amanda called. "Indians. In those hills. They're going to ambush the wagon train." The man stared in bewilderment while Amanda told him about the Indians. By the time she had finished, the man who had stopped the train galloped up to them. He was a tall man, and loomed so high above Liz that she had to tip her head back to see him. He was wearing a frontier suit that looked just like Tom's, but Tom's was nicer. Tom's had pictures of horses and Indians on the pockets.

"What's going on here?" he asked.

The first man turned to him and shook his head. "They say there are Indians in those hills, Daniel."

The tall man looked down at them sternly. Liz moved a step closer to Keechie. Then the man threw back his head and began to laugh.

He looked down at Keechie. "What's your name?"

"Keechie."

"Well, you listen now, Keechie," the man said. "You and your friends git right on back to your maw. And if I ever catch any of you out in front of this train again, or up to any other silly tricks, I'll sell the lot of you to the Indians. We got scouts out to look for Indians, and we don't need any help from you. Now git."

The tall man turned and waved and shouted to the wagon train. The wagons started forward again, and the two men on horseback rode off in front of it.

Amanda stamped her foot angrily. "Well, of all the stupid idiots! I guess we'll just have to let them be massacred."

"My kitty!" Keechie wailed. The kitten, tired of being clutched to Keechie's chest, had leaped out of her arms and was running away toward the hills where the Indians were hiding.

"My kitty!" Keechie cried again, and ran after it.

"Keechie, come back here!" Liz called, but Keechie didn't hear her. She and the kitten darted in front of the first of the passing wagons. Liz and Amanda managed to squeeze through between the second and third, but they were too late. Keechie was already climbing up the hill.

"Keechie, Keechie, stop!" Liz called. She and Amanda ran toward the hill.

The kitten was leading Keechie higher and higher. Finally the kitten stopped in front of a big rock near the top. Keechie approached the kitten cautiously. Liz heard her calling, "Here kitty, kitty, kitty." The kitten crawled up into Keechie's arms and licked her chin. Keechie snuggled the kitten and sat down on a rock to wait for Liz and Amanda.

Liz sighed with relief, only to hear Amanda call, "Watch out, Keechie!"

An Indian was stalking Keechie. Suddenly he swooped down, caught her and the kitten up in his arms, and disappeared over the top of the hill.

"Keechie, come back here!" Liz called. She and Amanda ran as fast as they could to the top of the hill, but the Indian was already far down the other side.

"Oh," Liz said, and she and Amanda sat down on one of the rocks. "What will they do with Keechie?"

"Scalp her, I guess," Amanda answered. "Or burn her at the stake."

"Oh, Amanda, I knew we should have stayed at home."

"Never mind. We'll just have to rescue her."

"Yes," Liz said, "that's what we'll do."

"We'll track them." Amanda took the canteen off her shoulder, and both girls had a long drink in preparation for their ordeal. Then Amanda rose. "Come on," she said, and set off. Liz followed confidently along behind. Though she worried about Keechie being lonesome and about their being late for supper, she was perfectly sure that if she just kept walking along behind Amanda they would eventually catch up with the Indians.

"Is it much farther?" Liz asked, finally.

"Maybe we'll see them when we get up the next hill," Amanda said. They marched steadily up the hill, and when they got to the top, they saw a large Indian camp spread out below.

"Let's get closer." Amanda waved Liz forward and they crept down the hill. When they were close enough to see the details of the camp quite clearly, they hid behind the rocks.

"We better stay under cover," Amanda said. "They may have guards out."

Liz could see the Indian men sitting in front of the teepees and the Indian women tending the kettles that boiled over the fires. There was a group of children playing at one side of the camp.

"There's Keechie." Amanda pointed. The bright gold of Keechie's hair stood out clearly in the cluster of black-haired children. Keechie was sitting on a small black-and-white horse, and her pony tails bobbed merrily as an Indian girl led her around.

"Why, she's not scalped at all," Liz said, and looked at Keechie resentfully. While she watched, another Indian girl ran up with something in her hand. She offered it to Keechie. Keechie laughed, and put it in her mouth.

"She better get back here," Liz said. "I'm hungry."

"Well, we might as well eat too," Amanda said.
"We'll have to wait until it gets dark. Then we'll sneak
into the camp and find Keechie." Amanda set the canteen on the rock and pulled the box of soda crackers
out of her pocket. Liz helped herself to crackers.

"Mama doesn't let us stay out after dark," Liz said.
They both ate another cracker.

"Well, then we'll just have to attack," Amanda decided. "Give me the guns." Liz ate hurriedly while
Amanda loaded the guns. "I guess we'd better sur-
round them."

Suddenly all the dogs in the Indian camp went wild.

They dashed back and forth between the tents, barking crazily at a small striped animal.

"It's Keechie's kitty!" Liz said. "The dogs are going to get it."

"No they won't," Amanda said. "Not when they find out it's really a tiger in disguise." The kitten ran up the hill toward them, leading the pack of yapping dogs. The dogs had almost caught up when the kitten jumped behind a rock. The leaders of the pack stopped and became quiet. Then the first dog howled in horror. Over the noise of the dogs came a ferocious roar, and over the top of the rock, a huge tiger. It landed in the middle of the pack and slashed out viciously with its claws. The dogs turned and fled howling back toward the Indian camp. With easy pounces and occasional snarls the tiger nipped at their heels.

"Come on." Amanda jumped up and rushed after the tiger, shooting off her gun and shouting at the top of her voice. Liz followed, shooting her gun and shouting loyally, even though she was afraid she might hurt somebody.

The Indians, unnerved by the uproar, stood panic-stricken as the first of the dogs entered the camp. Several Indian children were knocked down, while others joined the excited pack. The Indian mothers ran after their children and the Indian fathers ran after the mothers. Together, dogs and Indians fled the camp with the snarling tiger pouncing along at their heels.

When Liz and Amanda arrived, all was quiet and deserted.

"How will we find Keechie now?" Liz said. She sat down to open her gun and straighten the roll of caps, and then around the corner of a tent came the black-and-white pony with Keechie on its back.

"Oh, there you are," Amanda said.

"Yes," Keechie replied, unconcerned by the riot that had just passed her by.

"Keechie," Liz said, "weren't you scared to be captured by the Indians?"

"Was I captured?" Keechie asked.

"Yes," Liz said. "Were you scared?"

"No," Keechie said. "But next time I will be."

"Well, we've got to go home now." Amanda got up.

"No," Keechie said. "I don't want to." She kicked the pony in the ribs and trotted away from them. Amanda leaped after her and got hold of the pony's bridle.

"We've got to," Liz insisted. "Before the Indians come back."

"No." Keechie started to cry. "I want to stay here. Let go of my horsie."

"We have chocolate cupcakes for supper," Liz said.

"Oh." Keechie stopped crying.

"With candy sprinkles on top," Liz said.

"Chocolate candy sprinkles, Lizzie?"

"Yes."

"All right," Keechie said.

"Let's ride the horse back to the time machine." Amanda climbed up behind Keechie and pulled Liz up behind her. "Giddap," Amanda shouted, and the pony trotted off. They went in the same direction as the Indians, the dogs, and the tiger, and Liz wished the horse would go a little slower. She didn't want to catch up with any Indians. Before long, she recognized the pass where the wagon train had gone, and then she peeked out from behind Amanda's back and saw the time machine in the distance. The pony trotted up to the time machine, and stopped. The time machine was surrounded by Indians.

"Oh, dear," Liz said. The three girls slid slowly off the pony's back, but the Indians paid no attention to them. They were all watching the time machine. One of the Indians approached it with spear poised. He danced up, reached out with his spear, and then backed off again.

"Well, come on." Keechie led the way forward. "If you want to get home." The Indians parted in front of the girls and let them through. Keechie, with Liz and Amanda behind her, marched up to the door and stepped in. The Indians gasped, and fell back from the time machine.

"Turn it on and let's get out of here," Amanda said. Liz pressed the switch, and Amanda took the steering wheel. The blue light filled the time machine, and Liz saw a small striped shape come out of a corner and rub against Keechie's leg.

"My kitty," Keechie said, and picked it up lovingly.

The light grew bright, then faded and disappeared. The girls stepped out just in time to hear Mrs. Dunn calling, "Tom, Liz, Keechie, supper's ready."

Liz and Keechie walked slowly toward the house, and Amanda turned toward the patio wall. Tom came wheeling in the gate on his bike. He looked at the girls suspiciously and then carefully inspected the time machine.

"I don't want any of you fooling around this. Because I'll be sailing around the Cape any day now."

"Yeh," Amanda said. "Send me a post card." She laughed, and swung up and over the wall.

Liz and Keechie went into the house.

"Go and wash your hands," Mrs. Dunn said. "I've been calling you for ten minutes. Where have you been?"

"Oh," Keechie said, "we were riding a horsie and captured by Indians and everything."

"Keechie," her mother said sternly, "don't tell stories."

"But, Mommy . . ." Keechie said. Liz took her firmly by the hand and led her away toward the bathroom.

6 New Shoes

"John, dear," Liz's mother was saying, "do you have to play golf every Saturday?"

Liz forgot to hurry with her egg; she forgot about Amanda sitting on the kitchen stool waiting for her; she began to listen to what her parents were saying. Her father didn't look up from his breakfast.

"Yes," he said.

"But, John," Mrs. Dunn continued, "I told you last week that I made a doctor's appointment for Mike, and you promised to look after Liz and Keechie."

"I know," Mr. Dunn said. "But I forgot. I'll tell you what I'll do. I'll get one of the boys to pick me up. Then you can have the car and take Liz and Keechie with you. They'd love to go."

Liz looked at Keechie, but Keechie was busy spooning the yolk out of her fried egg; so far she had managed to leave the white undisturbed. Liz looked at Amanda, but Amanda continued to gaze into space.

Mrs. Dunn sighed wearily. "It's out of the question. You've simply no idea what it's like trying to manage a baby and two small children downtown."

"Mama," Liz said, "then we could get my new shoes."

Keechie lost interest in her egg, and looked up. "I want some new shoes," she said.

"You see," Mr. Dunn said. "If you get the shoes on the same trip, it will save you a lot of time."

Liz was not reassured by the way her mother smiled. "Yes," Mrs. Dunn said. "And then I can spend the time recuperating from my nervous breakdown."

"Mrs. Dunn," Amanda said, "if you want, I'll go along and take care of Liz and Keechie."

"Splendid," Mr. Dunn said. "Amanda can watch them while you're in the doctor's office."

"Oh, splendid," Mrs. Dunn said. "And who'll watch Amanda?"

Liz's father took a final gulp of coffee, and got up from the table. "Well, since it's all arranged," he said, "I'll go call and get someone to pick me up."

"All arranged!" Mrs. Dunn exploded. "Now see here . . ." But Liz's father had already left the room.

"Well, then," Amanda said, walking quietly toward

the door, "I'll just go tell my mother, and then I'll come back and help Liz and Keechie get dressed." Amanda closed the kitchen door firmly behind her.

"Goody!" Keechie jumped down from her chair and hopped across the kitchen. "We can go."

Liz looked uncertainly at her mother, who was leaning slackly against the kitchen sink. "Mama," she said softly, "we ate almost all our breakfast and we drank all our milk, except Keechie left just a little bit. Mama, shall we go put on a dress?"

Mrs. Dunn looked at Liz. "That's nice, dear," she said. Then she laughed. "Yes, go put on a dress."

All the way downtown, Mike sat in his car seat beside his mother and pointed out the passing cars. Liz knelt between Keechie and Amanda and looked out the back window of the station wagon. The children were not permitted to shout at the cars behind them, but sometimes they made faces. Liz knew this was not proper, but she liked to see what the people in the car behind would do. Usually they paid no attention, but sometimes they laughed and sometimes they were embarrassed and looked away and sometimes they got very angry. Liz and Keechie liked it best when there were children in the car behind who made faces back at them. There were no children in the car coming up behind them now; there was only the man who was driving. As soon as he was close enough, the girls stuck out their tongues as far as they would go. The man looked startled; but then, as he pulled out to pass, he leaned 'way over toward them and stuck out his tongue. The girls sat back on their heels, and laughed.

"What's funny?" Mrs. Dunn asked. No one answered. Liz was watching a girl they were passing. She was about Liz's size and she was trying to ride a two-wheeled bike. Liz watched her until she was out of sight.

"Mama," Liz leaned forward, "could we go look at bikes? I mean, just to look, not to buy one until we have lots more money."

"We'll see," her mother said. Liz sighed. She remembered that, even more than she wanted new shoes, she wanted a red two-wheeled bike, a bike that was just the right size for her, much bigger than her tricycle but not quite so big as Tom's bike.

"Mama," Keechie said, "can we ride on the escavator?"

"If we have time and if you're a very good girl," Mrs. Dunn said, "and behave in the doctor's office." Liz's hopes of looking at bikes faded. Keechie never behaved in the doctor's office.

Mrs. Dunn parked the station wagon in the lot behind the medical building, and the girls clambered over the seat and out the door. By the time Mrs. Dunn had lifted Mike from the car seat, Amanda had each girl by the hand and was holding them firmly. They walked primly around the building to the entrance. Liz was careful not to step on any of the cracks in the sidewalk. Keechie skipped at every other step and tried to break away, but Amanda held tight to her hand. They went into the lobby, and Amanda stopped them beside the door that opened into the drugstore.

"Mrs. Dunn," Amanda said, "if you don't want us in the doctor's office, we can wait in the drugstore."

Mrs. Dunn's glance moved from the drugstore to Amanda.

"No," she said slowly. "I think you'd better come with me."

"We'd be quite all right," Amanda said.

"I may be gone awhile," Mrs. Dunn said. "You're sure that you can keep them out of trouble?"

"Oh, yes," Amanda nodded confidently.

Mrs. Dunn hesitated. Then she took out her wallet and handed Amanda a dollar bill.

"All right," she said. "You can get a soda. But don't leave this building. If I'm too long, come up to the doctor's office. It's on the third floor."

Amanda nodded, and Mrs. Dunn and Mike left them. Liz saw her mother watching them anxiously from the elevator; then the doors closed in front of her.

Amanda folded up the dollar bill and put it in her pocket. "Come on." She started for the door. "Let's go shopping."

Liz stared at Amanda unbelievingly. "Amanda," she said, "we told Mama we'd wait in the drugstore."

"She'll be gone at least an hour. We've got plenty of time."

Slowly Liz realized that Amanda had not had the slightest intention of waiting in the drugstore. "Mama said we weren't to leave the building," Liz said.

"She was only afraid we'd get lost or something. Mothers always worry about everything. Come on."

Amanda and Keechie were already out the door. Liz thought about going to tell her mother, but Keechie and Amanda would be gone by then and she might not be able to find her mother anyway. There seemed to be nothing else to do but follow. At first Liz held Keechie's hand and kept very close to Amanda. It was a busy day downtown; cars moved slowly past, bumper to bumper; people jostled each other on the sidewalk. A policeman blew his whistle, and on the curb a group of men in funny suits were playing music. Liz's chest felt tight and funny, just as if she were on her way to a birthday party.

"Where are we going?" Liz asked.

"There." Amanda pointed to the large department store across the street. The girls pushed through the people crossing the street and went into the store. They went around in the revolving door three times and stopped just inside.

"What shall we look at?" Amanda asked Liz.

"Bikes," Liz said. "And shoes."

"Dishes are always fun," Amanda said. "It makes the clerks so nervous."

Then Liz noticed that she had let go of Keechie's hand, and Keechie was gone.

"Where'd Keechie go?" Liz looked around, and saw her standing in front of the escalator. "Oh," Liz said, "Keechie wants to ride the escalator."

"Okay," Amanda said. "You go first. I'll help Keechie."

Liz stood in front of the escalator and watched it rise up from somewhere below. She studied the pattern of the steps to make sure she wouldn't step on a crack. She put one foot out and teetered forward and back, unable to decide on the proper moment.

"Well, go ahead." Amanda gave Liz a little nudge.

Liz plunged. Her timing was off, and the step split under her foot. She grabbed for the handrail, recovered her balance, and rode majestically upward. Liz glanced back. Keechie was holding Amanda's hand and solemnly watching the moving stairs. Amanda rode casually, one hand on her hip. Liz tried taking her hands off the rails, but just as she did, she reached the top and stumbled off. She waited to watch Keechie get off, and then moved on to the next flight. At the third floor they stopped to admire a wedding gown. By the time they reached the fourth floor, where they watched brightly colored poker chips swirl around in a washing machine with a glass front, Liz could ride no hands and get off and on the escalator without hesitating.

"Lizzie," Keechie said, "I wish we had an escavator."

"Yes," Liz agreed. "Instead of just an old stairway."

"Lizzie," Keechie said. "Maybe Mommy will buy us one when our stairs get worn out."

"Oh, Keechie," Liz said.

"Come along." Amanda led them past the washing machines and the stoves and the refrigerators to the skis and the tennis rackets. She picked up a basketball and threw it to Liz. Liz was going to throw it back when she saw a stern-faced salesman looking at them. She put the ball back and hurried on after Keechie. They found her sitting happily in a small fire truck. It was a beautiful bright red truck with real ladders on the sides and a platform behind for a passenger. Keechie pedaled it forward.

"Lookie," Keechie said. "Just right for me. I could ride you too, Lizzie."

"Keechie," Liz warned, "you're not supposed to ride them."

"Well," Keechie said, "I want to."

"You can't," Liz said, but then she saw a middle-sized two-wheeler in the stand beside Keechie. She walked slowly toward it. It was a beautiful silver color, and there were black streamers on the handle bars. Liz edged it out of the stand, and sat down on the black seat. If she stretched she could reach the floor with one foot at a time. A salesman appeared suddenly at Liz's side; he smiled pleasantly.

"Isn't that a little big for you?" he asked. "We have a smaller size, with guard wheels, that you could ride."

"I could ride this one," Liz said. "Tom taught me." She held up her arm to show the salesman the scar that ran up her arm from her elbow. "Eight stitches," she said.

"I'll take this one," Amanda said, wheeling an English racer up beside Liz. Amanda looked at Liz doubtfully. "That does look a little big," she turned to the salesman, "but I suppose that it'll be all right. Our bikes will be on stands anyway. Keechie's the only one who can really ride."

"It is not too big." Liz was indignant.

"All right," Amanda said.

"I think there's some misunderstanding," the salesman said. "I wish you could ride the bikes, but it's not allowed."

Amanda ignored him. "They said you'd help us put the bikes in the elevator."

"In the elevator!" the salesman said. "Who said that?"

"The man who fixes the window," Amanda explained. "And the other man. They couldn't come because they're putting up a guard rail so Keechie won't crash through the window. I hope it's good and strong. Do you think it will be?"

"Oh, I'm sure it will be," he said. "You mean the store window? You're going to be in the store window?"

"Can you steer that car all right, Keechie?" Amanda asked.

"Oh, yes." Keechie pedaled the truck in a neat circle around them. "See?" she said, nodding her head approvingly. "I can ride a car very well."

"Well, I guess we better get going," Amanda said. "The other man—I guess he's the manager or something—said we were to hurry. Our hour has already started. I guess he doesn't want to lose any money." Amanda started to push her bike toward the elevator. The salesman reached out and took hold of the fender.

"You're supposed to take these bikes down to the store window for a display?"

Amanda looked at him thoughtfully. "Do you think a dollar an hour is enough? That's what he said he'd pay us. But I don't know. That might be enough for Liz and Keechie. They're pretty little. But don't you think I should get more?"

"Yes, yes. A good deal more," the salesman said.

"Would you tell him that?"

"Tell who?"

"The man who hired us," Amanda said. "The manager, I guess."

"No," the salesman said. "I think you'd better tell him."

"Oh, all right." Amanda pushed the bike forward.

"You just help us get them all in the elevator," she said to the salesman. He kept his hand on the fender of Amanda's bike as he walked along beside her. "Maybe you could come and see us," Amanda said. "But I suppose you'll be too busy selling bikes. All the kids will be sure to want a bike when they see us, won't they?"

"I'm sure they will," the salesman said. "If you'll wait here, I think I'll just go and call . . ."

"Oh," Amanda said, "they said we should get a hat for Keechie. You know, a fireman's hat. In the Toy Department. Are the toys on this floor? Maybe you'd come and tell them what we want. I don't think they would give it to us."

"No," the salesman said, "I don't think they would." The salesman led the way; Amanda and Liz pushed their bikes behind him, and Keechie pedaled in the rear. When they came to the Toy Department, the bike salesman called the clerk over.

"Miss Graham, do you have a fire chief's hat for this little girl? These girls are going to display the bikes in the store window."

"Oh, what a clever idea!" Miss Graham said. "I've just the thing." She hurried away and returned in a moment with a bright red fire chief's hat. She put it on Keechie's head, and Keechie patted it carefully in place.

"Isn't she darling?" Miss Graham smiled, and the procession started off for the elevators again. The bike salesman buzzed the elevator and backed Keechie's car in with Keechie still riding in it. He arranged the bikes beside the car, and Liz and Amanda squeezed in.

"I suppose one of us should go with them," the bike salesman scratched his head.

"I'm all alone on the floor now," Miss Graham said.

"Well, I suppose I—" the bike salesman began.

"Come and see us if you get a chance," Amanda called cheerfully, and pushed the button. The elevator doors closed.

"Amanda," Liz said, "nobody hired us to ride bikes in the window."

"No," Amanda agreed, and they rode down to the second floor. The door of the elevator opened, and Liz looked out at the crowded floor.

"Amanda," she whispered, "look at all those people. They'll catch us and put us in jail."

"No," Amanda scoffed. "We're too young. Come on."

Keechie had already pedaled out and was making her way into Ladies' Millinery. Amanda rode off after her. Liz heard startled cries and excited voices and she followed reluctantly. A lady carrying a tall stack of hats screamed, and jumped out of Keechie's way. The hats spilled all over the floor, and Liz shivered a little as she rode through them. Keechie and Amanda cleared a path through Ladies' Lingerie and Women's Coats and Dresses.

They came to a broad aisle running the length of the floor. At the far end was a huge mirror with a rack of suits standing in front of it. They lined up across the aisle, and Amanda reached down and plucked a long umbrella out of the stand beside her. She pointed it at the rack of suits.

"Forward!" she cried, and they pedaled down the aisle as fast as they could go. They watched themselves come closer and closer in the mirror as they charged the clothes rack. Amanda and Liz swerved and stopped beside the mirror; Keechie charged under the rack and stopped two inches in front of the glass. She jumped out of the truck and ran back to pick up her hat.

"Did you see me?"

"We could do better," Amanda said, and led them off in a wide circle through Men's and Boys' Wear. They paid no attention to the people they passed, and the noise on the floor did not bother them. It always seemed to be coming from somewhere behind. Suddenly a siren screamed behind Liz, and Keechie pulled up beside her.

"Lookie, Lizzie! It really blows." Keechie planted her finger firmly on the siren. "Want to try it?"

Liz reached down and pressed the button quickly, then hurried on. They arrived again at the wide aisle with the mirror. Keechie stopped beside the umbrella stand and picked out a bright red one. Liz looked longingly at the umbrellas, but knew she couldn't hold one if she was going to steer the bike properly.

"Now, all together," Amanda said. "Charge!"
She started off at breakneck speed, with Keechie,
pedaling as hard as she could, behind her. Liz jumped
on her bike, and followed. The aisle was lined with
people. Liz wondered how Keechie could steer her
truck, hold onto the umbrella, and still blow the
siren. She tried to see as she turned out to pass,
but a man jumped into the aisle and began waving his arms. Liz swerved to avoid him, and grazed
the legs of a dummy in a striped bathing suit. The

dummy teetered and fell slowly into the man's arms and Liz crashed headlong into the rack of suits. The rack tipped over, and Liz and Keechie were buried in a pile of clothes. Liz dug Keechie out from under a pink linen suit and stood up to see a group of excited men coming down the aisle toward them. Leading the group was the salesman from the Bicycle Department.

"I think it's time to go," Amanda said. She seized Keechie's hand and headed for the escalators. Liz followed, trying to unwrap the sleeve of a bright yellow suit from around Keechie's neck. Keechie screamed in protest, twisted away from Amanda, and ran back to her fire truck.

"Come on, Keechie," Liz called. "You can't take that."

Keechie ignored them. She dragged the truck out from under the pile of clothes. "I need it," she said, and got in.

Liz could see that there was no use in arguing with her. The men were almost to them. She jumped on the back of the truck and pushed with one foot as they charged off for the Down escalator. Liz leaped on first, and Keechie followed, banging and clattering in her truck. Amanda brought up the rear, leaving her open umbrella at the head of the escalator for a roadblock. Liz sat on the front of the fire truck, Amanda stood on the platform, and Keechie drove them crashing down. By the time they reached the bottom, Keechie was blowing the siren again. The crowd of people at the bottom scattered in front of them, and they rode straight through, into the revolving door. As they entered, a fat lady pushed in from the outside. The door moved fast, the truck jammed, and they all stopped. There was an opening about a foot wide to the outside. The fat lady began to bang on the glass and shake her fist at them. Keechie stared at her for a moment.

"That's a fat lady," Keechie said, and jumped out of the truck and slipped through the opening to the outside. Liz and Amanda squeezed through after her. They could still hear the angry cries of the lady in the revolving door as they hurried across the street and passed unnoticed into the Medical Building.

Liz leaned against the wall beside the door to the drugstore, and Keechie, panting heavily, sat down on the floor beside her.

"Do you think they'll chase us, Amanda?" Liz asked.

"No, they're too busy getting that lady out of the revolving door."

"Weren't you scared, Keechie?" Liz asked.

"I'm hungry," Keechie said.

"Want a soda?" Amanda reached into her pocket.

But just then the elevator door opened, and Mrs. Dunn came out carrying Mike. She hurried over to them.

"Oh, dear," she said, "I'm so sorry it took so long.

Did you get terribly tired waiting, Keechie, dear?"

"Yes," Keechie said.

"Too tired to go look for shoes?"

Keechie hopped up brightly. "Oh, no."

"All right," Mrs. Dunn said. "You've been such good, patient girls." She led them out onto the street. Liz glanced apprehensively toward the store they'd just come from. There was a large crowd in front, and Liz thought she could hear the voice of the bike salesman.

"I wonder what that crowd is outside of Blackwell's," Mrs. Dunn said.

"Probably a sale," Amanda said, and Mrs. Dunn led them off in the opposite direction. They walked a block down the street and into a shoe store. Liz sank into a chair and propped her feet up on the salesman's stool. She was glad to sit down, but shoes, even new shoes, didn't seem very exciting any more. When the salesman stopped in front of her and asked brightly if she was going to get some new shoes today, she stared at him coldly.

"We'd like to see some saddle shoes," Mrs. Dunn said, and then, pointing to Keechie, "and some canvas shoes for this one."

Liz submitted indifferently while the salesman measured her foot, but Keechie jumped up eagerly. The salesman disappeared into the rear of the store and returned carrying two boxes. He stopped in front of

Keechie and took a pair of bright blue canvas shoes out of the box.

"Shall we try them on?" he asked, reaching for Keechie's foot. Keechie immediately tucked both feet under her and sat on them. She looked at the shoes thoughtfully.

"I would like some party shoes," she said.

"No, darling," Mrs. Dunn said. "You don't need party shoes. You need some shoes to play in. So let's try these on and see how they feel."

Keechie sat firmly on her feet.

"No," she said. "I want black shoes with pointy toes."

"These shoes have nice rubber soles," Mrs. Dunn said, "so you can run and climb and won't fall down. Party shoes have slippery soles, and you'd hurt yourself."

"No, I wouldn't." Keechie looked down at Amanda's black patent-leather shoes. " 'Manda never falls."

"She's bigger than you," Mrs. Dunn said, but Keechie continued to shake her head. "Perhaps," Mrs. Dunn turned to the salesman, "you can start with Liz."

The salesman moved his stool over in front of Liz and produced a pair of saddle shoes from the second box. Liz sat up.

"Mama, I want party shoes too."

"Liz," her mother tried to explain, "we're getting

you saddle shoes to wear to school. You can't wear party shoes to school."

"Amanda wears them all the time."

"I'm sure she doesn't wear them to school." Mrs. Dunn was firm.

"I don't have any others," Amanda said.

"I want some." Keechie began to sniffle.

Mike, who had been sitting patiently on his mother's lap, looked at Keechie curiously and then began to cry.

Mrs. Dunn bounced him against her shoulder. "There, there, dear. You're getting hungry, aren't you?" Mike continued to cry.

"We happen to have some very nice patent-leather shoes on sale," the salesman said.

"All right," Mrs. Dunn sighed. "We'll just look at them."

"My mother always says," Amanda put in helpfully, "that there's no point in buying shoes you don't like and won't wear."

When the salesman returned, Keechie held out her feet promptly. The man buckled the strap, and Keechie danced to the mirror and stood entranced, watching her feet. Liz could hardly wait to get her shoes on. She had never seen anything so shiny as their gleaming toes. The toes were as pointy as she had hoped, and there was a little buckle with glittering beads.

"Oh, Mama," Liz said, "aren't they beautiful?"

Mrs. Dunn smiled. "How much are they?" she asked the salesman.

"Six ninety-five."

"Six ninety-five! I thought you said they were on sale."

"Marked down from eight ninety-five," the salesman said. "It's a really good shoe."

"No, I'm sorry girls," Mrs. Dunn said. "It's out of the question. I don't even have that much money." To prove it, she took out her wallet. "You see, I only have thirteen dollars and some change. I can't get them for you."

Amanda reached into her pocket. "I've got a dollar."

"No, Amanda, I couldn't borrow your money."

"Oh, it's quite all right," Amanda said.

"Yes, Mama, please," Liz said.

"Mike, do stop crying," Mrs. Dunn said. "Your father would have a fit if I spent that much money on shoes."

"He wanted them to get shoes," Amanda said.

Liz saw her mother's eyes narrow slightly. "That's right. He did, didn't he?" she said. "All right." She took the dollar from Amanda. Amanda reached into her pocket again and brought out a sucker. She took off the paper and handed the candy to Mike. He popped it into his mouth, and smiled.

"Will they wear them?" the salesman asked.

"Yes," Liz and Keechie answered together.

Mrs. Dunn shrugged, and went to pay for the shoes while the salesman put the old shoes into the boxes and handed one to each girl.

Liz skipped out of the store. Her feet had never felt so light. She listened to the click of her heels on the sidewalk.

"Well," Mrs. Dunn said, when they were settled in the car, "do you like your shoes?"

Keechie sighed. "I like them the best of all."

Mrs. Dunn backed the car out of the parking lot. "That's good," she said. "I'm sorry you had to wait so long that we didn't have time to ride the escalator or anything. Perhaps we can leave Mike behind some-day and come downtown just for fun."

Liz looked at Amanda, but Amanda was staring straight ahead.

"Mama," Liz said, "I'm going to pick up my room every single night without you even telling me." And this time Liz knew that she was really going to do it.

7   The Sugar-Plum Tree

Liz finished buckling on her roller skates, and stood up. Her feet slid out from under her and she caught herself on the knob of the back door. She pulled herself up and stood quite still, looking apprehensively at her feet. Then she gave herself a little push, and coasted to the nearest chair. She hung on it a moment, then pushed off again. Half skating, half falling, she reached the post on the far side of the porch, and clung to it. Triumphant, she looked at Keechie and Amanda, who were sitting on the porch swing.

"You try it, Keechie," she said.

Keechie looked down at her feet. Weighted down by skates, they dangled an inch above the floor. "I already did," Keechie said.

"That was pretty good, wasn't it, Amanda?" Liz asked.

"Uh," Amanda muttered. Then she added, "There's not enough room here."

"I wish Mama would let us skate in the hall," Liz said.

"Maybe she will, Lizzie," Keechie answered.

"No, she won't. I already asked her." Liz thought a moment. "Why don't you ask her, Keechie?"

"All right," Keechie forgot about her skates and jumped off the swing. Her feet skidded out from under her and she sat down hard. "Ow!" she said, and lifted her head and bumped it on the swing. "Ow!" she said again, and in a fury began to tear off her skates.

Liz, afraid that Keechie might change her mind about asking permission, hurried over to help her. She patted Keechie on the head and pulled her to her feet.

"Go ask Mama," Liz said, and they all went into the house.

Liz's father and mother were sitting at the dinner table with the newspaper spread out before them.

"Mama," Keechie began, "can we skate in the hallway?"

"No, dear," Mrs. Dunn said. But Liz hardly heard; she had lost interest in skating in the hallway. There was something about the way her mother and father were talking and looking at the paper.

"Where are you going?" she asked.

"Just to the movies, dear," Mrs. Dunn said.

"Gee," Liz said, "you always get to go out. We never do. I don't want any old baby sitter."

Mrs. Dunn glanced apprehensively at Keechie. "Now, Liz," she said quickly, "we won't be gone long."

"Are we going to have a baby sitter?" Keechie asked pitifully. "Mike will cry."

"Mike won't cry unless you get him started," Mrs. Dunn said. "And you won't because you're a big girl now, aren't you, dear?"

"No," Keechie said. "I'm just a little girl. I'm just three years old. I want you to put me to bed."

"I'll put you to bed before we go. And I'll see if Mrs. Green can come and take care of you. You like Mrs. Green, don't you?"

"No," Keechie said.

"We don't like any baby sitters," Liz said. She saw her mother begin to fidget nervously; and then Amanda spoke.

"I'll baby-sit them, Mrs. Dunn."

"Oh, that's very nice, Amanda," Mrs. Dunn said. "But I think we'd better get someone a little older."

Mr. Dunn looked up from the newspaper for the first time. "How much do you charge?" he asked.

Liz watched breathlessly while Amanda walked past the table and into the living room. Amanda sat down beside Mike, who was on the floor surrounded by his blocks. Amanda piled up a tower of blocks; Mike reached out and swatted at it; the tower spilled across the floor.

"Oh, about fifty cents an hour," Amanda answered.

"Fifty cents an hour!" Mr. Dunn said. "That's robbery. I'll give you a quarter."

Amanda began to build another tower for Mike. "I'm very good with children."

"Oh, all right," Mr. Dunn said. "I'll make it thirty cents."

"John," Mrs. Dunn protested, "I don't think Amanda's old enough. And just to save a little money . . ."

"We'll only be gone a couple of hours," Mr. Dunn said. "The kids'll be in bed. Amanda's perfectly competent, and, after all, her mother's right next door."

Liz could contain herself no longer. She rushed over to her mother and jumped up and down at her knee. "Yes, Mama, yes, yes, yes," Liz said. "Please, Mama, let Amanda baby-sit us."

"Well . . ." Mrs. Dunn hesitated.

Keechie came and stood at her mother's other knee. She looked up solemnly. "Mike won't even cry if 'Manda baby-sits us," she said.

"I'll go speak to your mother, Amanda," Mrs. Dunn said. "But, John, you'll have to pay her at least thirty-five cents. I won't have you exploiting the child."

At eight o'clock, Mr. Dunn called, "Let's go," and

went out the door and got into the car. Mrs. Dunn came hurrying down the stairs.

"Liz and Keechie, you're not even in your pajamas yet. If you want me to put you to bed . . ."

"I want 'Manda to put me to bed," Keechie said.

Mrs. Dunn looked skeptically from Keechie to Liz to Amanda. "I think I'd better put you to bed."

"No," Keechie said. "I want 'Manda to put me to bed."

Mr. Dunn blew loudly on the horn of the car. "You go ahead," Amanda said. "I can put them to bed."

"All right," Mrs. Dunn said. "Mike's asleep. If he wakes up—which I'm sure he won't—there's a bottle in the refrigerator. Just heat it a little." Liz watched her mother flustering about, giving Amanda instructions. "Tom is watching TV at Jim's. He should be home soon." Amanda sat quite still on the sofa and nodded her head from time to time. Finally Mr. Dunn came back into the house; he took his wife by the arm and led her away.

Liz went to the window to watch them go. Then she wandered back and sat down beside Amanda. "I don't want to go to bed yet," she said. Suddenly there was a terrible racket in the hallway, and Keechie came shooting down the hall on her roller skates. She looked about wildly for something to grab, but her feet shot forward again and she sat down, skidding the rest of the way. She crawled to the living-room rug and got up laughing.

"I can do it, Lizzie," Keechie said. "Almost."

"Keechie, Mama said we were not to skate in the hallway."

"Well," Keechie said defensively, and sat down and began to take off her skates. " 'Manda," Keechie asked, "do you have any candy?"

"No. Do you, Liz?"

"No, Mama won't buy candy any more because Tom and I had cavities."

"I would like some candy, 'Manda," Keechie said.

"We could buy some if we had some money," Amanda said. "But I don't. Do you?"

Liz shook her head sadly. "No," she said. "Tom has lots of money, but he wouldn't give us any. Tom sells things and gets lots of money. Could we sell something?"

Liz looked hopefully at Amanda. Keechie jumped up and ran out of the room. She was back in a minute.

"We could sell my dolly." She held up the doll. There was a good deal of hair missing, and one eye was punched in.

"I don't think we'd get much for that," Amanda said.

"Well," Keechie said, "Tom sold a football."

"He had two," Liz said, "and he sold one to Jim, and got a lot of money."

"What could we sell?" Amanda looked around the room.

Suddenly Keechie jumped up again. "I know what," she said, and ran upstairs. She came down carrying two small boxes. "Daddy has lots and lots of these." She held out the boxes. Each box contained three new golf balls.

"Good!" Liz clapped her hands together. "Daddy got them for his birthday, and he already has a lot."

"I don't think it's quite the same as having two footballs," Amanda said.

"Oh, its all right," Liz said. "Daddy doesn't like them. He got them from Grandma, and he said if only she'd just send the money. He'd be glad if we could sell them for him."

"And, 'Manda," Keechie said, "I do want some candy. And bubble gum."

"I wonder who would buy them?" Amanda asked.

"Mr. Wilson," Liz answered. "He was here when the balls came and he said he liked that kind best of all. He lives just down our street a ways."

Amanda got to her feet and dropped the two boxes of balls into her pocket. "Okay," she said. "You go and fix the buggy. I'll get Mike." Liz and Keechie ran out to the porch. Liz straightened the blanket in the buggy and sent Keechie back into the house to get another blanket to use for covers. They were ready by the time Amanda came out carrying Mike. Mike cried when Amanda put him down in the buggy, but he stopped as soon as she started to push him.

"Let's go," Amanda said, and they went out of the yard. "Which way, Liz?"

Liz turned toward Mr. Wilson's house, and led the way. The moon had not come up yet, and the night was very dark. They walked straight down the street for two blocks; then Liz slowed down and began to examine the houses carefully. They looked strange. The trees and shrubs cast dark shadows, and the houses looked much bigger and older than Liz remembered. She stopped in front of the next walk and examined the house closely.

"Is this it?" Amanda asked.

A light came on suddenly in one of the upstairs windows, and Liz saw a baldheaded man standing in front of the window. She knew that wasn't Mr. Wilson. Liz shook her head, and walked on. She didn't want to have to tell Amanda that she didn't know which house it was. She stopped again at the next walk.

"Well," Amanda asked again, "is this it?"

Liz looked at the house doubtfully. She would have to tell Amanda.

"Yes." Keechie said. "It is."

"How do you know, Keechie?" Liz asked.

"Because there's Mr. Wilson's kitty cat."

Liz stared into the gloom of the yard and saw two eyes glowing out of the darkness.

"Here kitty, kitty, kitty," Keechie called. The cat approached warily and stopped a few feet away.

"Yes," Liz nodded. "It is, all right."

"I told you," Keechie said.

"Okay," Amanda said. "Now you two stay here. Keep out of sight and don't let Mike cry."

Keechie looked about. "I think I'll come with you."

"No," Amanda said. "You've got to stay and keep quiet or we won't get any candy."

Keechie sulked. "They don't have candy here. They only have apples."

"You've got to be quiet, Keechie," Liz said, "so Amanda can get the money to buy the candy." Liz led Keechie back behind the hedge and pushed the buggy up beside her. Mike started to cry again, and Liz pushed the buggy back and forth to quiet him. She stood on tiptoe and peeped over the hedge just in time to see Amanda ringing the doorbell. The door was opened by Mr. Wilson.

"Yes?" Mr. Wilson said.

"Would you like to buy some golf balls?" Amanda asked.

"Golf balls! What kind of golf balls?" He took the two boxes from Amanda and carried them into the hall to look at them under the light.

"What's 'Manda doing?" Keechie stood on tiptoe, but she wasn't tall enough to see over the hedge. She sat down in disgust. "I'm tired of waiting."

"Sh-hh," Liz whispered. Mike began to cry again. "Be quiet, Mike," Liz said. "Keechie, you push the buggy."

"No," Keechie said. "I'm too tired."

Then Liz heard Mr. Wilson's voice again and ran back to look over the hedge.

"Where'd you get these balls?" he asked.

"Oh, they were a birthday present," Amanda said. "My father doesn't play golf."

"So he gave them to you? Well, yes, I'll buy them. I'll give you a quarter apiece."

"They're very good balls," Amanda told him.

"Hm-mm, yes," Mr. Wilson said. "Well, how about thirty-five cents?"

"They're brand new."

"Okay, fifty cents apiece. But that's my final price."

"That'll be three dollars," Amanda said.

While Mr. Wilson got out his wallet, Liz squatted down beside Keechie. "She got it, Keechie. She got it." Liz heard the door close, and in a moment Amanda appeared, holding the dollar bills in her hand.

Keechie jumped up. "Now can we get some candy?"

"Come on," Amanda started off, briskly pushing the buggy. Liz and Keechie had to run to keep up. They had only a few blocks to walk until they came to the drugstore. They parked the buggy and clustered around it. Mike grinned up at them cheerfully.

"He's wide awake," Liz said.

"We'll have to take him in." Amanda picked Mike up and carried him into the drugstore. The store was a blaze of light. Liz looked around, waiting for someone to ask why she wasn't at home in bed. But no one paid any attention to them. They stopped to look at a watch suspended in a bowl of water; Liz and Keechie each gave the stand of paperback books a whirl, and then moved toward the candy counter. The counter of penny candy was five feet long, and just level with Keechie's nose. Each kind of candy had its own separate bin.

Liz walked down the row, looking carefully into each bin. Keechie snatched up a sucker and then reached for the bubble gum. She paused.

"Can I have a sucker and a round bubble gum?"

Amanda nodded.

"Both!"

"Yes," Amanda said.

Keechie got the bubble gum and then saw the Tootsie Rolls. "Can I have a Tootsie Roll? I'll save it until after supper."

"Yes," Amanda said.

"A Tootsie Roll, a sucker, and a bubble gum?" Keechie asked incredulously.

"Keechie, you can have lots," Liz said. "Can't she, Amanda? About fifty-nine."

"Fifty-nine!" Keechie repeated ecstatically.

Liz looked up from the row of candy for the first time, and saw the clerk watching them uncertainly.

"Did you girls want something?" she asked.

"Yes," Amanda said. "We want a bag. Two bags. Two big bags."

"You do have some money, don't you?" the clerk inquired.

Amanda produced her three dollar bills and waved them at the clerk, who hurried away after the bags.

Amanda gave one bag to Liz and one to Keechie. "There," she said. "You can each get 150 pieces. No, 149." Amanda picked out a sucker and a piece of bubble gum. She upwrapped the sucker and gave it to Mike and sat down on the floor to chew the gum and look at the magazines. Liz turned her attention back to

the candy counter. Keechie was working rapidly. Her
hand flew between the bag and the candy. She held her
bag out to Liz.

"Is that 149, Lizzie?"

"Oh, no," Liz said. "That's not hardly any." Liz
started systematically at one end of the row. She started
with suckers, and put one sucker of each color into her
bag. She put in ten Tootsie Rolls and three tiny boxes
of candy cigarettes. She came to the wax bottles of pop
and put in one of each color. She put in five bubble

gums and a bag of candy corn and a bag of M&M's and jawbreakers and tiny candy bars and more suckers and three pieces of licorice and some mints, and then she went back to the beginning of the row and started over again. At first Liz tried to count carefully, but she got confused in the middle of her first trip down the row. When she started her second trip, she gave up counting altogether and at the end of the row she carried her bag over to Amanda.

"I forgot," Liz said. "Are there thirty-five or forty-nine?"

"Seventy-six," Amanda said. "Get some more licorice for me."

Liz went back to the counter. Keechie was standing in front of the candy-covered bubble gum, slowly dropping the gum into her bag one piece after another.

"Don't get just bubble gum, Keechie."

"Well," Keechie said, "I like it the best of all."

Keechie looked at the bin. There were about half a dozen pieces left. Keechie put one more into her bag.

"You can have the rest, Lizzie." She held out her bag to Liz. "Do I have enough?"

"I don't know. You better ask Amanda." Liz went up and down the counter filling her bag. She found caramels and malted-milk balls and nuts and she even took some gumdrops, though she didn't like them very much. She made no attempt to count, now; she just watched contentedly as the level of candy rose in her bag. Each time she went down the row, she found it a little harder to decide what she wanted. Finally she carried her bag back to Amanda.

"One hundred and forty-two," Amanda said. "Get seven more."

Liz stopped in front of the first bin and put seven suckers into her bag. The bag was full to the top, and Liz had to hold it carefully to keep the candy from spilling out. Liz sat down beside Amanda to wait for Keechie. She did not take her eyes off her bag.

"Let's see, Keechie," Amanda called. She looked at Keechie's bag and then carried it over to the cash register and put it up on the counter. Liz put her bag beside Keechie's. Amanda placed the three dollar bills on the counter.

"Two hundred and ninety-eight," she said to the clerk. "And we ate two."

The astonished clerk looked at the bags and then at the girls.

"What are you going to do with all this candy?" she asked.

"Eat it," Keechie said.

The clerk got another bag, and began to count. By the time she reached one hundred there were several people waiting in line behind the girls. The clerk picked up the bags and handed them to the girls.

"Oh, here," she said desperately. "Don't eat it all at once."

"Oh, no." Liz was shocked at the idea.

"We're going to wait until after supper," Keechie said.

They carried Mike and the candy out to the buggy. They tucked the bags into the foot of the buggy and stood looking into them, making their first decisions slowly. Mike got another sucker; Amanda took several pieces of licorice; and Keechie started on bubble gum. Liz didn't want suckers or gum or anything that took a long time to eat. She chose a Tootsie Roll. The girls ate steadily all the way home. Liz made sure that she got at least one piece of each kind, and by the time they reached home she was happy to have a sucker that took a long time to eat. They rolled the buggy up on the porch and gathered around the bags. There was still a lot of candy left.

"I think I will have just one more bubble gum." Keechie reached into her bag.

"Amanda," Liz said, "where will we put all this candy?"

"You better hide it."

Liz shook her head sadly. She was sure the bags were too big to escape her mother's notice. "Mama would find it. She finds everything. Or else Keechie would tell."

"No I wouldn't, Lizzie."

"I know," Amanda said. "We'll make a sugar-plum tree."

"A what?" Liz asked.

"What's a sugar-plum tree, 'Manda?" Keechie asked.

"Why, it's a tree full of candy and bubble gum and all good things."

"Yes," Keechie said. "Let's make one."

"Can we?" Liz asked.

"Sure," Amanda said. "Go get some string."

Liz brought the string, and they carried the bags of candy over under the pepper tree. Amanda showed them how to tie pieces of string to the candy and then tie the candy onto the tree. She climbed high up and tied her candy among the topmost branches. Liz and Keechie climbed after her. Silently the girls scrambled up and down; occasionally stopping to eat a piece of candy. By the time they had finished, the moon was high in the sky. They stood under the tree and looked up at it. The cellophane wrapping on the candy caught the light of the moon and the stars, and glittered down on them. The tree was covered with dancing candy, and the light wind rustled the paper and whispered a soft message of sugar plums.

"Isn't it beautiful?" Liz sighed.

"Is it a really sugar-plum tree, Lizzie?"

"No, Keechie," Liz said. "It's not a really sugar-plum tree. But it's a sugar-plum tree, all right."

"Come on," Amanda said. "You've got to get to bed before your mother gets home."

Mike was fast asleep in the buggy, and Amanda scooped him up and carried him into the house and up the stairs to bed. Liz and Keechie trailed behind. When Amanda set Mike down in his crib, he opened his eyes, and wailed. Amanda popped his sucker back into his mouth, and he closed his eyes and went back to sleep.

Liz and Keechie went on into their room. Liz undid the buttons on Keechie's dress and helped her un-buckle her shoes. They had just got their clothes off, when Liz heard the car come in the driveway.

"Hurry up, Keechie!" Liz said, and frantically threw clothes out of her dresser drawer as she searched for pajamas. Liz couldn't find any of Keechie's, but she found two pairs of her own and hastily buttoned Keechie into one of them. She pushed Keechie into bed and climbed up into the top bunk. Amanda came in, turned off the light, and switched on the night light.

"Now pretend you're asleep," she hissed, and hurried downstairs. Liz heard the back door open.

"Be sure you keep your eyes closed, Keechie."

"Lizzie," Keechie said dreamily, "I would like an-other sucker." Then she yawned, and went to sleep.

Liz heard soft voices below and then footsteps as her mother and Amanda came up the stairs. Liz closed her eyes when she heard them in Mike's room. Next they came into her room.

"What a mess!" Mrs. Dunn said.

Amanda made reproachful clucking noises. "I told them to put their clothes away."

Mrs. Dunn walked over to the beds. "Fast asleep, the little dear," she said. Liz felt her mother pulling the sheet up over her. She kept her eyes tightly closed.

"Did they go right to bed, Amanda?"

"Well, they were a little hungry," Amanda said. "So they had something to eat first."

The back door slammed, and Tom bounded up the stairs. He came whistling cheerfully into Liz's room.

"You're late, Tom," Mrs. Dunn said. "I was just going to call." Then her voice became stern. "What is that in your mouth?"

Liz opened her eyes just a crack and peeked down. Tom was standing in the doorway. He reached up guiltily and removed a large sucker from his mouth.

"I thought we agreed that we weren't going to buy any more candy," Mrs. Dunn said. "Lord knows, you complained enough about all those trips to the dentist."

"Gee, Mom, I know, and I didn't buy it. I was coming into the yard, and it fell off the pepper tree and hit me on the head. So I thought I might as well eat it."

"Now really, Tom. I suppose it grew on the tree."

"I don't know, Mom," Tom said. "But that's just what happened."

"Well, you certainly don't lack for imagination."

"Probably he sees too much TV," Amanda said, and followed Mrs. Dunn out of the room.

Tom aimed a kick at Amanda's ankle. Amanda turned fiercely and kicked him back. Tom limped out holding his shin.

Liz climbed softly down from her bed and crept to the window just as Amanda came out of the house and swung up to the patio wall. Amanda stood up and reached high into the tree and plucked off a candy cane. Gently Liz raised the window.

"Amanda," she called, "will there always be candy?"

Amanda looked up at Liz and then at the tree. "I guess," she answered softly. "If you can find it."

8   At Home

Liz sat in the middle of the wading pool and pulled her swimming suit out, away from her stomach. Water filled the space between stomach and suit. Liz patted the suit happily.

"Look at my big belly, Keechie," she said. Keechie didn't look. She lay in the water, holding onto the side of the pool, and kicked her feet furiously.

"You're splashing me," Liz said. "Let's play shark."

"No," Keechie said. "I'm playing with Redo."

"Well," Liz said, "she can play too."

"No. She doesn't want to. She wants to see me dive." Keechie hopped up out of the pool and ran across the yard. She stopped in front of the wall, and turned.

"Watch out!" she called. "Here I come." Keechie raced across the yard, hurled herself through the air, and belly-flopped into the wading pool.

Liz looked at her admiringly. "That was good, Keechie. Doesn't it hurt?"

"No," Keechie said. "Not hardly at all. You do it, Lizzie."

"No, sirree." Liz plunged her head under the water and went round and round the bottom of the wading pool. She came up for air. "Look out," Liz called. "I'm a shark and I'm going to get you."

Keechie fled shrieking to the other end of the pool. Liz chased her until she heard shouts from the alley and the noise of the gate slamming. Tom and his friends, Jim and Wally, came into the yard. Wally had his BB gun slung over his shoulder and was carrying something cupped carefully in his hands. The boys hurried to the porch.

"What have you got, Tom?" Liz asked. Tom ignored her and went into the house. He came out carrying a ball of string. The three boys clustered around the table on the porch. Liz and Keechie looked at each other and then jumped out of the pool and went slowly toward the porch. Keechie squeezed up to the table; Liz peeked in between Tom and Jim. Wally was holding a large green beetle.

"Ladybuggie," Keechie announced.

"It's a June bug," Tom said disgustedly, and tore off a length of string and handed it to Wally.

"You hold it," Wally ordered. "And don't lose it." While Tom held the June bug, Wally slipped the string under the bug's wings and tied it around its legs. Liz watched Wally anxiously.

"Why's he doing that, Tom?" she asked. "He'll smother it."

The boys paid no attention.

"Okay," Wally said. "You can let go now." Wally looped the string around his hand, and Tom released the June bug. It took off with a tremendous whir, and circled around and around at the end of the string.

"Wow, look at it go!" Jim said.

Liz ducked behind Tom. The bug flew in furious circles, making a loud buzzing noise. Wally swung the string down lower, and the June bug banged into the table and settled there.

"Let me have it, Wally," Tom said.

"No, I want to," Keechie said.

But Wally swung the string away from the table. For a moment the June bug hung there limply. Then it began to fly again, buzzing loudly at the end of its string.

"It's a dive bomber," Wally said, and swung toward Keechie. The June bug grazed Keechie's head, and Keechie ran back to the wading pool.

"Stop that!" Liz said, and Wally swung the bug at Liz. It missed her nose by an inch, and Liz retreated to join Keechie beside the wading pool. Then she saw Amanda sitting on the patio wall.

"They've got a June bug," Liz called. "Come and see."

Amanda swung down and came toward the pool. She was carrying a shoe box with small holes punched in the lid. She walked to the pool without glancing at the boys. She set the box down a foot away from the pool and took off her shoes. Then she sat on one of the corner seats and put her feet into the water.

"What do you have, Amanda?" Liz asked.

"Oh, nothing."

" 'Manda's got one too," Keechie called to the boys. "And it's bigger." Keechie jumped into the pool, letting her feet slide out from under her so that she plopped down with a splash.

The boys looked Amanda over once and began to move away.

"Come on," Tom said. "Let's go catch some more."

"Let's get a whole bunch," Jim said, "and tie them all together. I bet if we got enough and tied them together, they could carry something."

"Well," Wally said, "it's pretty hard to catch one. I don't know if anybody could catch a whole bunch."

"Anybody can catch a June bug," Amanda said.

"Oh, yeah?" Wally said. "I bet you haven't got one. I bet you haven't got anything in that old box."

"Didn't say I did," Amanda said.

Keechie began to jump up and down in the pool. " 'Manda's is bigger. 'Manda's is bigger," she sing-songed.

130

Liz jumped into the pool, making the biggest splash she could. "And it can fly faster," she called. "And it makes more noise."

The three boys edged closer to the pool.

"I bet," Wally said. Suddenly Jim darted forward, grabbed the box, and ran to the other side of the yard. He set the box on the ground, and the boys stood around it.

"Give it back, or I'll tell," Liz called.

Amanda sat perfectly still. "You better not open it," she said.

Wally reached out with his foot and kicked the box. The box tipped over and the lid fell off. Four or five small yellow shapes darted out. One of them lighted on Wally's foot.

"Ow!" He howled. He dropped the string that held the June bug, and crouched over his foot. Then he rushed over and plunged his foot into the wading pool.

"It was a yellow jacket," Tom said.

"You let the June bug get away," Jim said.

"Well, it stung me," Wally said. "Ow!" he continued to moan in pain. He looked at Amanda accusingly. "It was a yellow jacket."

"I told you not to open the box," Amanda said calmly.

Tom and Jim came over to inspect Wally's foot.

"You better get a Band-Aid," Liz said.

"Ah, it's all right, I guess," Wally said. "Let's go

swimming." He began to roll up the trousers of his levis.

"No," Liz said, and sat down possessively in the middle of the wading pool.

"Yeah, let's," Jim said. "I'm hot."

"No," Liz repeated. "It's just for girls. You're too big and you take up all the room."

"And you make too many splashes," Keechie said.

"Ah, so do you," Tom said. The three boys rolled their pants up above their knees and lined up side by side at one end of the pool. They walked down the pool kicking their feet and sending up a shower of splashes. Waves of water rolled over the ends of the pool. Amanda left her seat and went over to the swing, shaking out her wet dress. Keechie turned her back on the boys and huddled in one corner of the pool. Liz jumped out. "Stop that!" she shouted.

The boys laughed, and continued to walk up and down, sloshing more and more water out of the pool. Then Wally, tired of that game, sat down on one of the corner seats.

"Where could we get an inner tube?" Wally asked.

Keechie jumped up screaming. "You're sitting on Redo!"

"I'm not sitting on anybody," Wally said.

Keechie started to cry. "He's sitting on Redo," she sobbed.

"Make him get up, Tom," Liz said.

Embarrassed, Tom whispered to Wally, "You better get up."

"What for?" Wally said. "I'm not sitting on anybody. Who's Redo, anyway?"

"Oh, she's not anybody," Tom looked more and more embarrassed. "But Keechie thinks she is."

"Is she nuts?" Wally asked. He looked curiously at Keechie, who was still crying.

"Mom says it's an imaginary playmate," Tom said. "Mom says lots of little kids have them."

Wally looked confused. "She's nuts," he said, but he got up and moved to another seat. Keechie stopped crying.

"I guess," Tom said.

"I never had any imaginary playmates." Wally looked at the other boys accusingly. "Did you?"

"Not me," Jim said.

"Heck no," Tom said. Liz opened her mouth and looked at Tom in astonishment. Tom dropped his eyes guiltily, and Liz decided not to say anything. "You know how girls are," Tom mumbled to his friends.

"Yes," Wally said. "They're all crybabies." He stretched out his legs, kicked his feet; and sent water splashing into Keechie's face. Keechie put her hands up over her face. Then she bent down and grabbed the hose that was still running water into the pool. She turned it full blast on Wally. He leaped up howling.

"Hey, look!" he yelled. "She got me all wet!"

"Ah, you were all wet anyway," Tom said. "Come on. Let's shoot your gun. Did you bring some BB's?"

"Yeah," Wally said. "But you guys should get your own."

The three boys walked to the porch in their dripping levis and got Wally's gun from the chair. Liz sat down in the pool again and watched them examine the gun. After some discussion, Tom brought an empty tin can out of the house and they set it up on the wall and began to shoot at it.

"You sure did fix him, Keechie," Liz said.

"Well," Keechie said, "he splashed."

"Come swimming with us, Amanda," Liz called. Amanda came back to the pool and sat down again.

"No," she said. "I'm busy." She put her feet in the water and made small whirlpools by wiggling her toes. "It's almost September," she said, "and I have to think about things." Liz looked at her enviously; she wished that she had things to think about.

The boys soon grew tired of shooting at the can.

"Let's play cowboys and Indians," Wally said. "We'll be the cowboys, and they"—he pointed toward Liz and Keechie and Amanda—"can be the Indians."

"No," Amanda said. "We're busy."

"They won't play," Tom said.

"Sure they will," Wally said. "Come on. We'll attack from behind the tree." He led the boys over to the pepper tree and they all crouched behind it. They peered out at the girls. Wally leveled the gun on them.

"We're not playing," Amanda said, and turned her back on the boys.

"Well, you better," Wally said, "because we're attacking."

Jim picked up a small clod of dirt and threw it at the girls. It landed in the middle of the pool. Liz watched the dirt dissolve and muddy the water.

"I'm going to tell Mama," Liz said. "And she'll take the gun away." Wally leaned forward from behind the tree and aimed the gun at them. Liz heard the report as Wally fired.

Amanda sprang up, clutching the back of her arm. She turned around slowly and looked at Wally.

"You shouldn't have done that," she said. Liz felt an icy shiver run up her back at the sound of Amanda's voice. Wally leaned forward and fired again. This time Keechie jumped up.

"You shooted Redo!" she wailed. "And she's dead!" She sprang out of the wading pool and started for Wally.

Amanda smiled. "Here, Keechie," she said. "Use this." She reached into her pocket, took out a stick about a foot long, and handed it to Keechie. Keechie took the stick and charged at Wally, waving it in front of her.

"Ow! Ow! Ouch!" Wally howled. He hopped on one foot and began rubbing his leg. Then he let go of his leg and grabbed hold of his shoulder. "Make her stop it!" he shouted.

Keechie halted a few feet in front of him. She stopped waving her stick, and looked at Wally in surprise. Tom and Jim were bewildered.

"What's the matter with you?" Jim asked.

"She never touched you," Tom said.

"Well, something sure did," Wally winced, and began rubbing his leg again. He grabbed his gun and glared at Keechie. "Get away from me," he said.

Keechie, remembering her stick, waved it at Wally and moved slowly toward him.

"Ow! Ow!" Wally called. "Help!" He dropped his gun and covered his head with both arms. Then he turned and ran. Keechie chased him out the gate and down the alley. In a moment Keechie trotted back through the gate. She stopped inside and leaned against the wall to rest. Tom went over and took the stick out of Keechie's hand.

"It's just an old stick," he said, and handed it to Jim.

"He must be nuts," Jim said.

"What did you do to him, Keechie?" Tom asked.

Wide-eyed, Keechie looked up at Tom. "Why, not anything at all. Just only chased him home." Then she looked at the wading pool. "Look out, Lizzie," she said. "Here I come."

Keechie ran across the yard, hurled herself through the air, and belly-flopped into the pool.

"That was a good one, Keechie," Liz said.

9 And Away

Liz looked mournfully around her empty back yard and went on into the house. Her mother hurried out to the kitchen to greet her.

"Well, here's my schoolgirl. And how was school today?"

"Where's Keechie?" Liz asked.

Mrs. Dunn persisted. "Did you have a nice time at school, dear?"

"All right," Liz said.

"Did you play some nice games?"

"Yes," Liz said, with no enthusiasm.

"Did you color some pictures?"

"Yes," Liz nodded. "Where's Keechie?"

"She's over at Amanda's. What else did you do?"

"Oh, I don't know," Liz said. "I think I'll go over to Amanda's." She started for the door.

Mrs. Dunn gave up. "All right," she said. "Do you want something to eat first?"

Liz came back into the kitchen and waited while her mother cut up an orange and handed down the cooky jar. Liz took three cookies and the quartered orange and carried them down the alley and into Amanda's yard. Keechie and Amanda were sitting on the floor of Amanda's porch. They looked up as Liz approached, and silently accepted the food she offered. Liz sat down beside them. In front of Amanda was a jar of paste and a big box of something that looked like wrapping from cigars. Amanda was pasting the brown scraps that looked like cigar wrappings into odd-looking balls. She wound the scraps around a large pencil, then put on paste and more scraps. When she finished, she took the pencil out and there was a hollow ball with an opening at one end. But Keechie's job interested Liz the most. In front of Keechie was a box full of things that glistened and sparkled. Liz could see sequins and beads and little bright buttons and scraps of silk and satin and bits of colored paper and tiny silver balls like the ones her mother put on cookies. When Amanda finished one of her balls, she handed it to Keechie, and Keechie filled it with the bright stuff from her box.

"What are you doing?" Liz asked.

" 'Manda's making cocoons and I'm stuffing them."

"Can I do some?"

"No," Keechie grabbed the cocoon in front of her. "I'm doing it."

"Well," Liz said, "I don't have anything to do."

"You could swing, Lizzie," Keechie said helpfully.

"I don't want to."

"You could swing," Keechie said, "or ride bikes or go home or play with the kitty or go home."

"Amanda," Liz said loudly, "I want to do some."

"Well, you could do lots of other things," Keechie said. "Not just sit there bothering us."

Liz turned on Keechie furiously, and Keechie ducked down behind her box.

"Here." Amanda handed Liz a finished cocoon. "And hurry up, you two. We have to finish these today."

Happily, Liz took the cocoon and reached deep into the box. She brought out a handful of tiny glistening objects and put them down in front of her. There were tiny bits of colored glass and colored cotton; there was green and pink paper grass from Easter baskets; there were many bits of fabric, some of them smooth and shiny, some of them soft and fluffy. They were like a butterfly. Liz began to drop pieces into the hole Amanda had left in the cocoon. She watched Keechie, and saw her fill the cocoon up to the top and then put it carefully on the pile beside her.

"Hurry up," Amanda said; Liz hurried and filled her

cocoon to the top. She shook it, and listened. There was a faint rustling. By the time Liz had finished, Amanda had another cocoon ready for her. The girls worked on, silently. Liz filled five more cocoons before she spoke.

"Amanda," she said, "why don't you go to school?"

"I've already told you."

"Yes," Liz said. "But everybody goes to school. My mama says."

"We're going to move. So I'm not going to start school here."

"Will you go to school after you move?" Liz wanted to get to the bottom of the matter. Amanda didn't answer her. Liz sighed, and went back to work. She had finished another cocoon before Keechie looked up.

" 'Manda," Keechie said, "I don't want you to move."

"I have to," Amanda said. "Now, don't talk to me. I have to work."

For almost ten minutes no one spoke. Then Liz said, "What are you going to do with all these cocoons?"

"I need them," Amanda said.

"Oh," Liz said.

"You'll see what for, tomorrow, if you want to come."

"I have to go to school tomorrow."

"Well, if you'd rather go to school, Keechie and I will do it."

"Yes," Keechie agreed. "We'll do it."

"No," Liz said. "I'd rather go with you."

"Okay," Amanda said. "Take your lunch to school,

and we'll meet you in the school yard at lunch hour. We'll be home by the time school's out, and your mother will never know the difference.

"Well," Liz said. She was quite sure that her mother would know the difference. Her mother had very carefully explained to her why everybody went to school. Even though her mother hadn't been quite right about Amanda's case, Liz knew that you couldn't just not go to school. Probably policemen came and put you in jail. But Amanda seemed to consider the matter settled. There were only a few scraps left in Amanda's box, and she concentrated on pasting them together. She finished the cocoon and handed it to Keechie. Then she stood up. A large burlap bag was leaning against the side of the porch, and Amanda brought it over to where Keechie and Liz sat.

"Here, Liz," Amanda said. "You hold this open."

Liz looked into the sack, and gasped. It was already over half full of cocoons. Liz held the bag open and Amanda dropped in the cocoons they had just finished, and the bag filled up to the top. It was as high as Keechie, and much fatter.

"There must be hundreds and millions of cocoons," Liz said.

Amanda tried lifting the bag. "It's pretty heavy," she said, "but I guess we can manage it. We'll take your wagon tomorrow."

Liz was very quiet that evening. She ate her supper uncomplainingly and even took two bites of carrots so that she wouldn't have to discuss the matter with her mother. She put away her coloring book when she was told that it was time to get ready for bed; she picked up her room without making too much of a fuss even though Keechie, who was responsible for most of the disorder, refused to help her. Liz was sure that if she got involved in any kind of discussion, her mother would guess that she was not going to school tomorrow afternoon. Just before she got into bed, Liz brought up the matter of lunch.

"Can I take my lunch to school tomorrow?" Liz looked up at the ceiling.

"Why, yes, dear, if you want to," Mrs. Dunn said. "Tom is going to take his lunch. You can eat with him."

This didn't worry Liz because she knew Tom always played ball at noon, and wasn't likely to insist that they eat lunch together.

The next morning Liz set off for school swinging her lunch box. It was a red-plaid lunch box and brand new. Liz didn't do well in school that morning. She was embarrassed once when the whole class laughed because the teacher had called her name twice and she hadn't even heard. When the bell rang at twelve, she hurried to the back of the room for her lunch box and went out into the school yard. Tom was not in sight, and Liz headed toward the farthest corner to avoid her classmates. There, on the corner, she found Keechie and Amanda waiting for her.

"Hurry up," Amanda said. "We don't have all day."

Beside Amanda was the big burlap sack bulging out over the side of the wagon. Amanda picked up the handle of the wagon, and started off.

"We been waiting and waiting, Lizzie," Keechie said as she and Liz fell into line behind.

"Where are we going, Keechie?"

"I don't know, but we have to hurry."

They hurried across streets and down many blocks and into the park. They hurried right past the play area, and Keechie looked longingly at the swings and slide. They followed Amanda and the wagon far out into the deserted area of the park. They climbed a little hill, and finally Amanda stopped under the mulberry tree that grew on top.

She took the sack out of the wagon and leaned it against the tree. She untied the top of the sack and took out a toy guitar. Suddenly embarrassed, Amanda looked over at Liz and Keechie.

"I don't sing very well," she explained, and began to turn the handle on the guitar. The guitar made scratchy, plunking noises. Amanda had played the song through twice, before Liz recognized "She'll Be Comin' 'Round the Mountain." Liz sat down on the grass; they had walked so fast that her legs ached. Amanda played soberly on her guitar and gazed off into the distance. Keechie walked over and stood very quietly beside Liz.

"What's that, Lizzie?" she whispered.

Liz stood up and saw something that looked like a

large patchwork quilt moving slowly toward them across the grass.

"I don't know, Keechie," Liz said. She glanced apprehensively at Amanda, but Amanda seemed to be expecting the strange thing flowing toward them. She watched it calmly, and continued to turn the crank on the guitar.

"I think we'd better be getting home, Lizzie," Keechie said; but neither girl moved. They continued to stare, and as the shape came closer, Liz could make out small creeping creatures.

"It's caterpillars, Keechie."

"Oh," Keechie said. "I like caterpillars."

The caterpillars slowly climbed up the hill. There were all kinds: fuzzy ones and knobby ones, fat ones and thin ones, green ones and brown ones and striped ones, fierce-looking caterpillars and caterpillars that looked as soft as pussy willow. The caterpillars spread out in a circle around Amanda and the mulberry tree. Liz sat down in the wagon and tucked her feet up under her.

"We might step on one," Liz said to Keechie, and Keechie sat down in the wagon and pulled her feet up too.

When the caterpillars had all gathered round, Amanda stopped playing the guitar. She tipped over the burlap bag and spilled out the cocoons in a wide circle all around the tree. When the bag looked empty, she held it up by the bottom and gave it a final shake.

"Okay," Amanda said. "But hurry up. We don't have all day." She went back to her place and began to play on her guitar. The caterpillars moved toward the cocoons. A large caterpillar with a stripe down his back and horns that stuck out over his head crawled purposefully through the cocoons until he came to one his size. He poked his head in and out of the hole, making up his mind. Finally satisfied, he gave a shake and wriggled into the cocoon.

"Amanda," Liz called loudly over the noise of the guitar, "caterpillars make their own cocoons."

"Nonsense," Amanda said.

"Yes, they do, Amanda. We have a cocoon at school. My teacher said a caterpillar made the cocoon and he was inside it, changing into a butterfly."

Amanda snorted. "If that's what you learn at school, I guess I'm not missing much."

Liz nodded. Amanda was probably right. She hadn't really believed her teacher anyhow. The caterpillars were still busy selecting their cocoons, and Liz realized she was very hungry. She opened her red-plaid lunch box and took out the sandwich. She ate the sandwich and shared the banana and the potatoe chips with Keechie. There were three cookies in the box. Liz and Keechie had one each, and Liz put the third back for Amanda. By the time they had finished eating, the caterpillars had all disappeared into their cocoons.

Amanda put down her guitar and began to gather up the cocoons and put them into the burlap bag.

"You can help," she said. "But don't squash any."

Liz got down from the wagon gingerly. She picked up a cocoon and held it carefully in two fingers, then dropped it into the bag. Since the caterpillar hadn't jumped out at her, she picked up another. Keechie was already stuffing whole handfuls of cocoons into the bag.

"I like caterpillars," Keechie said. When the cocoons were all gathered up, Liz and Keechie helped Amanda hoist the sack into the wagon.

"Are you going to take them home?" Liz wondered if Amanda's mother would allow her to keep all those cocoons in the house.

"No," Amanda said. "We're going to hide them."

"Why are we going to hide them?"

"So kids won't find them," Amanda said, "and take them all to school."

They visited all the areas of the park, and at first Liz had trouble finding hiding places, but before long she was seeing good places everywhere she looked. Amanda pulled the wagon out onto the golf course that lay right beside the park. Liz stopped at the edge. Every Saturday, when she asked her father if she could go with him, he told her that children were not allowed on the golf course. But there was no one in sight, and Amanda had already pulled the wagon across the dirt road and down through the ditch.

There were not many players on the course, and the girls stayed mostly in the rough. Several times they heard angry shouts when they had to cross a fairway, and Amanda would turn and stare indignantly at the golfers. Once a man driving a little car chugged up and demanded to know what they thought they were doing.

"Attending to our own business," Amanda said.

Cowed, the man backed his car off while he mumbled insults at their mother and the management of the golf course.

Once another man ran after them shouting, "Did you girls pick up my ball?"

"Of course not," Amanda said. "What would we want with your silly ball!" Amanda walked on, pulling the wagon behind her. Liz saw Keechie back away, her eyes round and her hands tightly clenched behind her back. Liz waited until they were safely away from the man.

"Amanda," Liz said, "Keechie's got his ball."

"Well," Keechie said. "I was just taking it home to Daddy."

Amanda shrugged, and Keechie tucked the ball into the wagon. There were many excellent places on the golf course. Liz was disappointed when Amanda wouldn't let them hide cocoons in the holes with the flags sticking out of them.

By the time they left the golf course, the burlap bag was three-fourths empty and there were about a dozen golf balls in the wagon. All the way home they hid cocoons. They hid them in cracks in walls and under stones and in hedges and trees. They had just reached their own block when Amanda took the last cocoon out of the sack.

"Can I have that one?" Liz said gently.

"Okay," Amanda said. "But don't take it to school."

"Lookie." Keechie pointed down the block. There in front of Amanda's house was a big moving van and Amanda's mother was calling and waving to them.

"Where have you been?" she asked, as they pulled up. "We're almost ready, and I've been looking all over for you."

Amanda followed her mother into the house. Liz and Keechie pulled the wagon into their yard and then climbed up onto the wall where they had the best view of Amanda's yard.

They saw the movers come out of Amanda's house, close up the van, and drive off. Next they saw Amanda come out of the house carrying a box. Amanda's black cat was in the box. Amanda put the box in the car and went back into the house. For a long time there was nothing to see. Then Amanda and her brother Billy came out.

" 'Manda," Keechie called. Amanda walked over to the wall where Keechie's kitten was sitting washing its face in the sun. Amanda picked up the kitten and carried it over to Keechie.

150

"Take care of my kitten," Amanda said.

"Yes, 'Manda," Keechie promised. "When are you going to come back?"

Amanda shrugged. "Oh, I don't know."

"Won't we ever see you again?" Liz asked.

"Maybe," Amanda said. "We move around a lot."

"You could come and visit us," Liz said, but Amanda shook her head.

"You've got to come," Keechie said.

Amanda's mother and father had come out of the house and were getting into the car.

"Come along, Amanda," her mother called. "We're going."

Amanda looked up at Liz and Keechie. "It's not so easy. But maybe I could come for Halloween. I'll try."

Solemnly, Liz and Keechie nodded. Amanda looked over the wall toward the gate where Tom had just entered the yard. He carried a long, homemade periscope. Amanda shook her head sadly.

"It'll never work unless he adjusts the transluped," she said. She turned away and walked to the car and got in. Tom sat down on the wall beside Liz and Keechie, and they watched the car drive down the street. Billy waved to them from the back window, but Amanda sat up straight and did not look back.

"There goes Amanda." Tom sighed, almost sadly.

"I thought you didn't like Amanda," Liz said.

"Oh, she was all right. For a girl."

"She's coming back for Halloween," Keechie said.

"She can't," Tom said. "Mom says they're going to Texas."

"Yes, she is," Keechie said indignantly. "Isn't she, Lizzie?"

Liz pushed past Tom and began to walk down the wall to the pepper tree. "Of course she is, Keechie," Liz said. "Tom doesn't know everything. Why he doesn't even know enough to adjust the transluped on his old periscope." Liz grasped a branch of the pepper tree and swung down to the ground.

10 Halloween

"Is it Halloween now, Lizzie?" It was the fifth time Keechie had asked that afternoon, so Liz tried to explain very carefully.

"First we have to eat supper," she said. "Then we have to put on our costumes and wait for it to get dark, and then it's Halloween."

Keechie thought for a minute. "Why can't we put on our costumes now?"

This seemed sensible to Liz. "We'll ask Mama," she said.

The girls arrived in the kitchen with their question, only to find that supper was ready. And though Liz and Keechie and even Tom were too excited to do much more than fidget, they all sat down respectfully at the table. There the Halloween plans almost met with disaster. Mr. Dunn declared that it was impossible to expect him to pass out candy to Trick-or-Treaters; Mrs. Dunn declared that it was unthinkable to allow Liz and Keechie to go out by themselves; and Tom declared it most unfair to burden him with Liz and Keechie, who were too little to keep up with him and his friends. The discussion became heated, Keechie shed a few tears and Liz began to whimper before a compromise was reached. Tom was excused from his Saturday chores, and in return he agreed to take Liz and Keechie out for an hour. Then he would bring them home and be free to go on with his friends.

"Okay, Mom," Tom finally agreed. "But you gotta make them hurry up."

Liz left the supper table and rushed upstairs to start getting dressed for Halloween. She had spent a great deal of time deciding what costume she would like. Every time she went to the store, she studied the row of costumes that hung on a line across the ceiling of the dime store. She finally settled on the gypsy costume because, while it didn't have a crown like the princess costume, or a wand like the fairy costume, it had three necklaces and four bracelets. But when Liz announced her decision to her mother, her mother said:

"Buy a Halloween costume? I should say not! Why, when I was a girl the fun of Halloween was in making your own costume."

Liz had pleaded and coaxed, and was still a little bitter with both Keechie and Tom because they wouldn't support her. Tom had decided to be a hobo, and Keechie wanted to be a ghost. Even when Liz had pointed out the princess costume and the clown costume to Keechie, Keechie had been firm.

"But, Keechie, you were a ghost last year," Liz said.

"I always want to be a ghost, Lizzie," Keechie answered. "I like ghosts."

Liz was forced to give up the gypsy costume, and since a homemade gypsy costume would not have been the same at all, she agreed when her mother suggested that she be a black cat. With her mother's help, Liz had made a mask with pointy ears and whiskers and a long swishy tail, and at the time these had seemed poor substitutes for three necklaces and four bracelets.

But now, as she pulled on her black tights and navy-blue T-shirt, she began to feel quite catlike, and rather pleased with herself. When her mother arrived to pin on her tail, Liz found that by wiggling a little she could swish it back and forth. She pranced around the room swishing the tail while her mother arranged Keechie's sheet. The girls put on their masks and ran downstairs to show their father, while Mrs. Dunn hurried off to make Tom a shoe-polish mustache.

Keechie waved her arms and fluttered her sheet. "Lookie, Daddy, I'm a ghost."

"I'm a cat," Liz said. She leaped nimbly up on the

sofa and from there to the arm of her father's chair. "Meow!" she said. Liz was sure that she must be a very savage cat because her father looked alarmed. She stopped leaping for a minute when Tom appeared in the living room.

"How do I look?" Tom asked.

"Nice, Tommy," Keechie said admiringly.

Liz looked at the dirty black stuff on his face. "It'll never come off," she said, and pounced across the room at Keechie's kitty, who skidded under the nearest chair.

"Ah, stop hopping around," Tom said. "We gotta go." The sound of voices from the street carried into the room.

It was seven o'clock, and quite dark outside when the first Trick-or-Treaters rang the bell. Mrs. Dunn hurried out of the kitchen with a bowl of candy in one hand and three large brown paper sacks for the children in the other hand. Tom opened the door.

"Hi, Tom. Come on, Tom," a chorus of voices called.

"I gotta take my sisters," Tom said apologetically as he rushed out into the crowd of boys at the door. Liz grabbed Keechie's hand and hurried after him.

"You look out for them now, Tom," Mrs. Dunn called, and was answered by several boys' voices shouting: "Sure. Okay. We will."

The boys stopped for a moment at the sidewalk to decide which way to go. Liz and Keechie stood several feet away, looking at the group suspiciously. Though one boy looked like a skeleton and another like a space-man, Liz was quite sure that they were the same boys who always came to play ball with Tom. Even so, she thought it best not to get too close. The boys started off whooping down the street. Tom yelled, "Come on," and Liz and Keechie followed at a safe distance.

They had just started up the walk to the first house when the last boy in line turned around, let out a loud whoop, and the eyes in his mask turned a bright green. Keechie shrieked, and darted behind Liz. The boys laughed.

"Ah, it's just Fred," Tom said. But Liz and Keechie stood where they were.

"Lizzie," Keechie whispered, "I don't like him." They watched the boys go up to the house, ring the bell, get their bags filled, and start off again. "Go on," Tom said as he rushed past them. "They give you candy bars." The boys ran on to the next house. Liz and Keechie stood on the walk and looked up at the house.

"Come on, Keechie," Liz whispered. Gripping Keechie's hand tightly, Liz moved toward the house. They approached the door.

"We've got to knock on the door," Liz said.

"I will." Keechie stepped forward and knocked. They stood perfectly still, and waited. The door opened on a large man holding a box. Liz opened her mouth but

no words came out. She swallowed, and then she opened
her mouth again.

"Trick or treat," she said faintly. The man's voice
boomed out at them, saying something about how small
the ghosts were this year. Liz didn't understand what
he was talking about, but it didn't matter because the
man reached into his box and brought out two candy
bars. He dropped one into each of their bags. Then the
door closed. Liz and Keechie stood and stared into their

bags. The candy bar was there, all right, a dark shape
at the bottom of the bag. Then they heard Tom come
running up behind them.

"Come on," he said. "You can't just stand around."

"That was easy, Lizzie," Keechie said, and they
turned and ran after Tom.

He hurried past the next house. "Never mind that
house," he said. "They don't have anything very good."
At the next house he paused, and stopped. "You better

go here. You get popcorn balls. I'll be right up ahead. But hurry up if you want to get a lot of candy and stuff." Tom ran on, and Liz and Keechie looked up at the house.

"I like popcorn, Lizzie," Keechie said. "Do you?"

Liz nodded solemnly and took hold of Keechie's hand. They advanced quietly and steadily like brave soldiers, and eventually reached the door. Liz knocked twice. They stared straight ahead, and waited.

"You better knock some more, Lizzie," Keechie said, but Liz couldn't. She had taken one step backward when the door opened.

A lady beamed out at them. "I thought I heard a tiny little knock," the lady said.

"Trick or treat," Liz said.

"If I don't have a treat, what kind of trick will you play?" the lady asked.

Bewildered, Liz stared at her.

Keechie looked up at the lady confidently. "Trick or treat," she said firmly.

The lady laughed, and produced two popcorn balls and dropped them into the bags. The door closed, and once more the girls stood and looked down into their bags. Liz still could not believe in the magic that made strange people come to the door and give them good things to eat.

"We better find Tom," Liz said, and the two girls ran out to the sidewalk, where they saw Tom running back to fetch them. He lectured them severely on the necessity of keeping up, as they ran to catch up to the group of boys who waited a few houses ahead. Liz and Keechie had both forgotten their fear of Fred and his green eyes, and this time they stayed close to the boys. They soon discovered that all they had to do was stand in line and hold their bags wide open, and the level of candy rose up and up. Liz soon lost track of what was in her bag, and Tom would never let her stop long enough to find out. Instead she shook the bag to hear the rattle. Keechie managed somehow to keep her mouth full even though Tom became angry every time she stopped to eat something.

By now, there were many children out. Small, ghostly figures fluttered across the lawns all up and down the street, and Liz had to stay close to Keechie in order to tell which ghost was Keechie. The night was full of noise. Several times Liz turned suddenly when someone called, "Hi, Liz," but she never found out where the voice came from. The laughs and cries of children mingled with the anxious calls of the mothers who prowled the street. Trick or Treat was the refrain Liz ran to. Her feet kept time to it; it pounded in her head and came automatically to her lips every time a door opened.

Liz ran and stopped and ran again; she laughed and even shouted; she was always surprised to find herself shouting. Lost in the night, she did not even recognize her house until Tom stopped and pointed.

160

"You better get home now, or Mom will be worried."

"No, Tom, not yet," Liz said, but she was ready to go home. She protested only because she felt it was her duty. Together with Keechie she followed Tom quietly across the street and up the walk to their house.

"Go on in now," Tom said. "And tell Mom I'll be home in a while."

They watched Tom run off, and then Liz said, "Let's fool Mama." They went up and knocked. Mrs. Dunn opened the door and stared sternly down at them.

"Trick or treat," Liz and Keechie said.

"You two have been here before," Mrs. Dunn said.

"No." Liz shook her head.

"Well, you certainly look familiar," Mrs. Dunn said.

Keechie began to giggle. "It's me, Mommy."

Mrs. Dunn bent down and looked closely at Keechie. "Why, so it is." She looked at Liz. "And who's this?"

Liz clapped her hand over her mouth to keep from laughing, and Keechie said, "It's Lizzie, Mommy."

Mrs. Dunn peeked under Liz's mask and then shook her head in amazement. "I guess it is, all right. No wonder you looked familiar. You'd better have a candy, since you fooled me." She dropped a candy into each of their bags.

"Mama," Liz said, "may we stay out a little longer? If we stay right here."

"All right," Mrs. Dunn said. "Just while I'm putting Mike to bed. But don't go out of the yard."

"We won't, Mama," Liz said.

Liz and Keechie sat down under the light beside the door to examine the contents of their bags. They spread all the candy out on the concrete, and counted and compared. Liz had a good deal more candy than Keechie because Keechie had eaten so much. They each still had a popcorn ball and decided to eat the popcorn balls together. Everything else went back into the bags. They went down to the end of their walk and sat down on the step. The Trick-or-Treaters were not quite so many now. Most of the little children had gone, but there were still groups of older children. They watched one group make its way down the street across from them. Once they had to move to let four girls go up and knock at their door. Liz heard the girls laugh at something her daddy said. When the girls were gone, Liz and Keechie sat down again.

"What's that, Keechie?" Liz pointed up to the moon. A strange object was floating toward them down the path of moonlight. It looked like a broom with someone riding on it. Liz got ready to run. "I think it's a witch, Keechie!"

"No, Lizzie," Keechie said. "I think it's just 'Manda."

Liz looked again. The figure came closer and passed near a street light, and Liz recognized Amanda's shiny black shoes with the white bows. It was Amanda riding on the broom with her black cat perched behind her.

She looked down at them, and waved. The broom glided to a gentle stop in front of the Dunns' house. Amanda dropped the broom and stood up, stretching. She glanced carelessly at the bags they both held. "Got any licorice?" Amanda said.

Liz and Keechie reached into their bags and rummaged around until they found some.

" 'Manda," Keechie said, "I would like to ride on a broom."

"Isn't it scary, Amanda?" Liz asked.

"No," Amanda said, "but you do get kind of stiff." She stretched her legs out one at a time and shook them a little. "That's why I really don't like to be a witch on Halloween."

" 'Manda," Keechie said, "I would like to ride on a broom."

"Would you, Amanda?" Liz asked. "Would you take us for a ride?"

"Well." Amanda looked doubtful. "It's my mother's

old broom, and it's not very strong. I don't know if it would hold us all."

"Yes, 'Manda," Keechie said. "Please."

"I guess we could try it," Amanda said. "It might be all right if we don't go very high and if you don't wiggle."

Liz and Keechie jumped up, and Amanda arranged them on the broomstick. First Amanda straddled the broom, then Keechie, then Liz, then Amanda's black cat. "Ready?" Amanda asked. She tipped the end of the broom skyward and pushed with her feet. They began to rise gently. At first they flew only a few feet above the ground. "Too much weight," Amanda said, but she kept tugging at the end of the broom, and gradually they gained altitude. When they were almost on a level with the second-story windows, the broom lurched and began to dive. Amanda had to fight the end of the broom to get it pointed upward again.

"Liz," Amanda said sternly, "you've got to sit still."

"Well." Liz tried to stop squirming. "It's not very comfortable."

"Never mind that. Just sit still, and you'll get used to it."

Liz sat very still, though she didn't think that she could ever get used to it. "Do you like it, Keechie?"

"Yes," Keechie said. "I like *Halloween* the best of all. Do you like Halloween the best of all, 'Manda?"

"No," Amanda said. "It's just a bunch of little kids begging for candy."

"I like candy," Keechie said.

Amanda was expert at handling the broom despite its additional weight. She skimmed rooftops, swooped over telephone lines and dipped under power lines; she looped around chimmeys and circled around lampposts. Liz searched through her bag of candy until she found three pieces of bubble gum and distributed them to Amanda and Keechie. Liz chewed on her gum and tried blowing a few bubbles; she swung her legs and found that she wasn't so uncomfortable any more. In fact, she could sway easily with the curves of the broom. Once Amanda swooped down on a group of children and sent them shrieking and running in all directions. Liz felt a little sorry for the children. She was sure they thought they were being chased by real witches. They rode as far as the drive-in movie, and there Amanda flew them across the path of the projector. Liz watched as their shadows loomed, huge and terrifying, on the screen, Amanda's shadow first and then Keechie's with her sheets fluttering about her, then herself. Her cat's ears were a little crooked, but her tail hung down neatly, waving slowly below the broom. Amanda's black cat sat primly behind her. Amanda turned the broom and started back toward Liz's house. They had almost reached home when they saw four boys walking down the street. Amanda dived low over them. Keechie leaned far out.

"Hi, Tommy!" Keechie called.

"Sh-hh, Keechie," Liz said. She looked back over her

shoulder. Tom's startled face stared up at them. Liz
hoped Tom hadn't recognized them; he might tell
Mother that they'd left the yard.

Amanda glided the broom over the hedge and landed
Liz and Keechie at their front door.

"I've got to be getting back," Amanda said.

"Amanda," Liz said, "you come next Halloween, for
sure."

"We'll get you some more licorice," Keechie said.

Amanda shrugged. "Okay, if we don't move to Washington." She tipped up the end of the broom, and sailed off.

Liz and Keechie stood and watched until they saw Amanda fly across the path of the moon, and then they went into the house. Mrs. Dunn called to them from upstairs.

"Hurry on up to bed now, girls. It's late."

Liz and Keechie went rather wearily about the business of undressing. They heaped their clothes up in the middle of the room and crawled into their pajamas. Liz complained a little when her mother insisted that they brush their teeth, but she was too tired to care very much. She put her bag of candy away in her drawer and climbed into bed. As her mother was turning off the light, Liz heard Tom come in. He hopped up the stairs and met his mother just outside Liz's door.

"Where's Liz and Keechie?" he asked.

"Why, they're in bed, Tom."

"That's funny, I thought I saw them . . ." Tom's voice faded away.

"Saw them where?" Mrs. Dunn asked. "What's funny?"

"Oh," Tom said, "nothing, Mom." Liz sat up in her bed. Tom paused, then looked in the door of the room and went away shaking his head. "Not anything, Mom," he said.

Liz sighed and lay back down. She hadn't really

meant to disobey her mother. She'd just forgotten about promising to stay in the yard.

"Lizzie," Keechie called sleepily from the bottom bunk, "when will it be Halloween again?"

"Well," Liz said, "next there's Thanksgiving and then Christmas and then Easter and then my Happy Birthday and then your Happy Birthday and then it's Halloween again."

"Oh," Keechie said. "That's not very long. I can wait that long."

Liz didn't say anything, but she knew that Keechie was wrong. It was a long time to wait. Liz looked wistfully out the window at the pepper tree shining in the moonlight, and when she fell asleep she dreamed that Amanda was sitting on the patio wall under the pepper tree—she was waiting patiently for Liz and Keechie to come and play.